Once Upon a Time in the West

"This gory Spaghetti Western reads like a barroom brawl between Sergio Leone, Robert E. Howard, and Quentin Tarantino with Elmore Leonard howling from the rafters. A bloody, naked Elmore Leonard, how's that for an image you can't unsee? Too much? Well, then too bad for you, ya lily liver. Because John Dover serves up a gorgeously nasty cocktail of resurrection and redemption riddled with bullet wounds and teeth marks...really big teeth marks. Don't be shy, step on up to the bar and knock it down."
-Charles Austin Muir, author of *Slippery When Metastasized* and *This Is a Horror Book*

"This book is fast paced, has vampires, demons, ghosts, shoot-outs, violence and a whole barrage of other dark, horrific delights to keep you entertained. There are some really original concepts that I have never come across before and the fact that I am a huge reader means that doesn't happen very often. John is a great writer, and this book will take you on a journey through the town of Thrall and further into the desert as foe chases foe and old rivalries are put aside to battle a common enemy."
-Kevin J. Kennedy - author of *Halloween Land* and Owner of KJK Publishing

"This is a visceral and indulgent Spaghetti Western romp. Dover's lush descriptions are a delightful contrast to the violent and harsh experiences of his

characters. The world Dover writes for Samuel, William, and Finn is nothing short of immersive. Smells of whiskey, blood, and dirt waft off of every page. This story moves from one deliciously gruesome event to the next at breakneck speed. Before you know it, you've finished the tale and read of innumerable dismemberments."
-Cora Y. – author

"John Dover's book, *Once Upon a Fang in the West*, feels like a gritty, dirty, "Spaghetti" Western with a great cast of characters. Now add Vampire's and other creatures and you have quite the mix. I couldn't put it down. I needed to find out who survives."
-Kelley Baker – independent filmmaker and author of *Road Dog, From Arrah Wanna to Mule Shoe*, and the upcoming *Dennis Barton Is A Bastard and Other Stories*.

"Dover's *Once Upon a Fang in the West* is a hilarious page-turner Western, as well as a very explicit, gory vampire tale that binds the genres. Just pour yourself a shot of whiskey and wear an apron before reading."
-Ivonne Saed, author of *Triple crónica de un nombre* (*Triple Chronicle of a Name*).

"The enemy of your enemy is supposedly your friend, right? But how far would you go to defend your town from a vile creature of unspeakable horrors when that 'friend' is an unsavory vampire? Find out in this fast-paced, pulpy tale of horror, gory deaths, and bloody dealings between a sheriff and unwanted visitors to his Old West town. A flesh-rending good time!"
-Rick Cook – author

"Visceral, vicious, twisty...a small-town sheriff's past haunts him as he joins forces with vampires on the hunt for...something worse. Once Upon a Fang in the West will have you checking dark corners and avoiding dark alleys. And never trusting a dead body."

-LeeAnn McLennan, author of *The Supernormal Legacy* (*Dormant*, *Root*, and *Emerge*)

"Can a story with this much blood and gore be called 'pure'? Because this is pure fun!"
-Benjamin Gorman, author of *Don't Read This Book*

"Rye whiskey, wry humor, and abundant gore—hold onto your ten-gallon hat for this thrilling, bloody ride!"
-Karen Eisenbrey, author of *The Daughter of Magic Trilogy*

"Four-fisted Western action: one to aim your gun, one to hold your whiskey, and two still (barely) attached to the severed arms of the supernatural baddies who dared to oppose our Big Damn Hero! Hilariously violent fun by a master of modern pulp!"
-Jason Brick, author of *Wrestling Demons*

"A gory good ride through a Wild West where the good guys are bad, the bad guys are worse, and everyone has a taste for blood."
-Nan. C. Ballard, author of the forthcoming *Under Carico's Moons Trilogy*

Once Upon a Fang in the West

by

John Dover

Once Upon a Fang in the West

Copyright © 2021 by John Dover

All rights reserved.

Published in the United States by
Not a Pipe Publishing
www.NotAPipePublishing.com

Trade Paperback Edition

ISBN-13: 978-1-948120-82-1

Cover art by Don Aguillo

To my wife, Jessica

Contents

Prologue — Ruby's World

The saloon stinks of blood, piss, and clumsy sex. God, it makes me hungry.

Off in the corner under the staircase, Hank assaults the keys — and our ears — from his raggedy piano. Behind the bar, Earl spills half the night's profits from his stock of lukewarm beer and paint-stripper he calls whiskey. And all through the room, the other girls work on ushering the local boys into manhood and luring the traveling cowpokes into more exotic locales of the flesh. Not my idea of fine dining, but the smell of seduction whets my appetite.

"Hey, Ruby." Earl puts down the glass he's swabbing with his crusty apron. "What'll I get for ya tonight? Your usual?"

"Double rye." I turn back to the room's thick tobacco haze and look for tonight's distraction.

"Who's buying?"

"I'll let you know."

Earl pulls out a passably clean glass and pours out a healthy double.

"Much obliged," I say. And just because this is our nightly routine: "Anyone interesting come in so far?"

"Mostly the usual crowd. But the one over there seems to be keeping to himself. You might take a crack at him if you're feeling the muse." Earl gives me a wink with his one working eye.

I look past Betsy and her bouncing cleavage at the stranger drinking at the center table. He sits with his legs stretched long and lean and his hat low on his brow. Sure enough, he looks promising. Give the one-eyed bartender some credit for pointing out fresh prey while I'm salivating over the same tired, greasy livestock that keeps the Braided Pony plodding along. Now that I'm onto the newcomer, I can't believe I missed the tang of his musk, the scent of danger on him unlike the usual oily stench of bad business in this place. I might as well get a less distracting view. I throw back half my glass, nod thanks to Earl and head to my lookout on the second floor.

Now I see how I had missed him.

His fluid movements are a blur to me, making him near invisible to the cattle that roam around him. He anticipates their clumsy moves and silently directs them around his space. He avoids the swing of a sloshing glass, leans away from hats lowered in drunken chivalry and dodges knives drawn for a brawl. His most conspicuous act is holding down his table when Jethro, two-hundred-and-fifty pounds of bristling ego, stumbles into it. Not even that lug budges it under his grip. He stares right through the cold gaze of the stranger before letting go of the table with his sausage-fingered mitts. The stranger seems to have a gift for not being seen or suggesting silently that he best be left alone. A gift like that serves only one purpose: To conceal an even greater power.

He could squash them like ants, but he chooses to live passively among them. I get it. It's never ideal to face an angry mob, pitchforks in hand and torches ablaze. mimicry has its benefits. Sometimes the other option is making a ghost town out of a well-stocked pantry of drifters. My enticement towards the stranger get distracted by the scent of another predator approaching the door. This must be my lucky week.

The scent is strong and less guarded than my stranger. I sharpen my gaze on the rickety door below. I shut out the rest of the room and listen to the footsteps tromping on the wooden planks on the other side.

The rusty hinges groan as tendril-like fingers wrap around the top of the weathered door. Silvery eyes scan the room from under a large-brimmed hat. They settle on my lonely stranger's table. The door swings open. A wash of cool night air mingles with the humid warmth of the saloon. A tall figure, flanked by two broad-shouldered mounds of trouble, enters. The leader's thin-lipped smile stretches across his face. His sharp features slice through the room as he moves toward the center table.

The air prickles with energy. I shiver with anticipation of the unfurling scene below. I swallow down a swig of rye and settle in for the show. If only the cattle knew what they were about to witness.

Chapter 1 – Dust-Up in the Saloon

Wrapped in black, flowing dusters, Samuel and his two goons wove through the crowd. Finn sat alone sipping his whiskey. The three men stopped at his table.

"Hello, Finn," Samuel said. "How have you been, my boy?"

"I'm not your boy."

"Still warm and welcoming, I see."

Finn answered with a quiet sip of his drink.

"Well...maybe not so warm afterall." said Samuel. "Our time apart has done little to improve your manners. There's no need to be rude."

"No need to hunt me down like a dog, either."

"More courteous than lighting you on fire in your sleep, I would imagine." Samuel traced a long finger down the pale scar on his cheek.

"What do you want, Samuel?"

"You know why I'm here. It's time to come home."

"Fuck off."

"Maybe later." Samuel winked. "Anyway...I think we have both had enough time to think about how things were left."

"I had hoped I left you a pile of ash."

"I'm willing to forgive and forget."

"But I'm not." Finn refilled his glass and took another sip. "You also know it won't be that easy to take me back, or you wouldn't have come here with your little posse."

Samuel's companions glowered.

"They are only here for training purposes, I assure you."

"You assure me shit. Now how about you and your lap dogs back off before we have a bigger problem than me spilling a couple drops of my drink."

"Mm. And such a fine vintage it must be." Samuel nodded at the half-empty bottle of hooch next to Finn's glass. "Let's keep this civil, Finn. Get up now and come with us."

"I'm pretty sure you and your boys are the ones who need to turn tail before I finish what I started back at the ranch." Finn slipped his gun hand under the table.

"We were hoping to keep this quiet."

No doubt sensing the mounting tension at the table, the crowd — and even the fellow torturing the piano in the corner — grew quiet.

A scowl darkened Finn's face. "I'm not the scared whelp you stole away with all those years ago, Samuel," he said. "I've learned a lot since the night I left you for dead. And I promise you I will be the one to walk out of this place, leaving you to burn on the pyre with the rest of the garbage."

"Pity, boy." Samuel looked down at his boots and shook his head. "I would have preferred to warm my bed with you tonight rather than lick your blood from my hands." He raised his eyes to meet Finn's. "But if that's what you want."

Finn nodded.

The tabletop erupted as Finn unleashed a hail of buckshot from below. His three would-be captors flew backwards, showered with buckshot, splintered table, and his shattered whiskey bottle. He jumped up, reloaded his sawed-off shotgun in mid-air and landed on the nearest goon. They hit the ground and Finn pulled his trigger. Bone, teeth, and brain matter smeared the floorboards.

"Walk that off, asshole."

Samuel roared and backed away. His enlarged canine teeth unsheathed and talons sprang from his fingertips.

"Tear his throat out," he said to the remaining, bloodied lackey who snarled and charged.

Finn readied another round, but Samuel's attack dog was faster than he anticipated. He slapped the barrel away as Finn pulled the trigger. Lead pellets peppered the wall. The goon unsheathed his fangs and chomped at the air like a rabid dog as they wrestled for control of the gun. His attacker's talons bore into the back of Finn's hands. Finn head-butted him. Blood sprayed from the man's nostrils and his eyes rolled into his head. Finn grabbed him by the back of the head and slammed him down onto the up-ended table. Its jagged leg exploded through his chest and he went limp.

Finn glared at Samuel. The dead goon's insides speckled his face. "Like I said, I'm not your boy."

Samuel frowned. "You have no idea the pain I'm going to rain down on you for your insolence, Finn."

Finn holstered his spent shotgun. "Let's finish this."

Samuel charged. Finn dodged left, crouched low and swept him up by his legs. He spun and tossed Samuel across the room towards the bar. The sharp crack of bone filled the room as he collided with the heavy oak and splashed down into a puddle of spilled beer. With a flying lunge, Finn landed atop Samuel's broken body with one knee on his groin. He drew his hand-carved Bowie knife from his belt and drove the wooden blade between Samuel's ribs into his heart. Samuel's eyes went blank. Finn knelt on top of his former master, satisfaction and relief washing over him as the last of Samuel's being oozed out onto the floor. Finn glanced around the saloon.

The piano started up again. The drunks, cowpokes, and working girls went about their business, unfazed by the speed with which Finn dispatched his three opponents.

After a moment, he climbed to his feet and grabbed an abandoned whiskey from the bar.

The slack-jawed bartender watched as he knocked it back.

"Barkeep," Finn said.

The bartender's handlebar mustache twitched. "Y-yes, sir?"

"I need a fresh bottle of whiskey. Also...," he nodded at the man running a broom across the floor on the other end of the bar. "maybe your boy should fetch a wheelbarrow and haul the bodies away for a proper burning. Don't want them stinkin' up the place now, do we?"

The bartender gaped.

"Well?" Finn said.

"Y-yes sir."

The bartender told his helper to do as Finn had suggested, then pulled a black bottle from under the counter.

"Much obliged," Finn said as the bartender uncorked the fresh hooch and pushed it toward him.

Finn took a drink. The heat settled in his gut. He spread ten gold pieces across the counter. "Sorry for the mess." He tipped his hat and moved off with his glass and fresh bottle in search of a quiet table to drink, comfortably removed from the slaughter strewn about the room.

Chapter 2 – Ruby Prepares for an Introduction

The regulars shrugged off Finn's carnage as the nightly entertainment, but Ruby was entranced by the gruesome display of virtuosic violence. Her knees quaked and the railing she held groaned under the pressure of her grip as she fetishized the spectacle from her perch. She gathered herself to go down to the main floor.

She descended the stairs and planted herself at the bar opposite Finn's table to eavesdrop on his exchange with the local sheriff. The sheriff said he wouldn't lock him up, but he wouldn't be welcome in his town after tonight. She would have to move quickly to gain his attention before one of the other girls swooped in for a taste.

She gestured to Earl for a drink. He obliged, and she choked down the spicy shot. A single tear surfaced and dropped to the bar. Earl chuckled. "You okay, Ruby?"

She exhaled the fumes and gathered her breath. "Just

fine, honey. Let it go down the wrong pipe is all."

"Oh, I bet you say that to all the boys."

"Only the ones with enough coin to get the wrong pipe." She winked wickedly as Earl nodded his knowing approval.

Ruby strategized and the rest of the world went on with its business as Roy and Slim returned with their cart to haul off the three dead bodies. The two bickering oafs grunted and squawked as they hoisted the heavy corpses onto their wobbly transport and hobbled their way out of the bar. They bounced through the rutted alleyways to deposit their cold passengers to the burn pile with the rest of the trash.

Chapter 3 - William's Walk, Part One

The pale sun painted the sky pink and purple as it dove for the horizon, making way for the moon's turn on watch. William stared into the cool evening sky as it settled over the valley. He was still sober enough to walk and talk straight, but the whiskey's warmth lubricated his movements as he patrolled the streets of Thrall.

William had few responsibilities in Thrall Township, aside from the occasional dust-up at The Braided Pony. There was no missus or ankle-biters waiting for him at the end of the day. He just had the title of sheriff, his drink, and his nightly walk.

When he was a bright-eyed youth, William built his name with a lightning draw and keen aim. He could clip the spurs off a cowpoke at fifty yards with little more than a blur from draw to re-holster.

William's legend, along with his ego, grew with each passing year, the gossip train expanding his mythic skills from county to county. The town adored their Adonis and warned any newcomers that if they were looking for trouble, William would make sure they left with a limp...or worse.

William's nightly ritual became the backdrop for the memories of his salad days. The days of fist-laden vanquish of arrogant braggarts who came to test their mettle. He delighted in the game and he never lost, and until Jesse showed up, he had never killed.

Jesse. All knees and elbows. Barely fourteen and already pushing six-feet, even without the untamed hair towering up in a gravity-taunting rooster tail. His voice cracked with the beginnings of a man's tenor. He should have been spending his free time playing doctor behind Pa's barn, but instead he had grown up reaching for his hip, aspiring to be the next William.

William's steps slowed at the conjuring of Jesse. No matter how hard he tried, Jesse arrived every night. William would notice the subtle itch at the back of his brain that signaled Jesse clawing out from the dusty murk of the past and into William's present. Night after night William thought, maybe it will be different tonight. He wanted to stop walking, but he couldn't. He was drawn through the streets, blinded by the summoning, never stumbling, never straying from the winding path until he stood face to face with Jesse again.

He walked past the Braided Pony, down the alley towards the church. Townsfolk greeted him as he glided past in an oblivious trance. He did not even notice the dark-clad trio that passed on their massive steeds.

Jesse consumed William's thoughts. Standing defiantly before him, a cocky smile painted across his face, his pa's dusty Peacemaker weighing down his sagging belt.

William crossed the growing shadow of the church. The off-key warbling from the early evening congregants serenaded passers-by with their latest hymn. William's trance broke for a brief moment as he stopped and listened, searching for sanctuary from his recurring hell. Their song finished, and they sat with a rumble while pastor Thomas began to preach. "Demons walk among us children. Be sure of that."

William continued on towards the barn.

Chapter 4 – William, Fifteen Years Earlier

William woke to the frantic thumps of oversized boots tramping across the wooden planks leading up to the sheriff's office where he slept at night. Jonah Samson burst through the door, breathless and sweating from his sprint across town. At nineteen, Jonah still dressed in the oversized hand-me-downs from his gargantuan brother, concealing his slight figure and giving him a much younger appearance.

"Sheriff, you gotta get out to the Black Cross Ranch right away!"

William squinted at the bright sunshine intruding on his morning slumber. "Slow down, son. What's the rush?"

"Graham says there's been a fire and he needs your help right away." Jonah blushed realizing William was not alone. A bare-assed, curly-headed blonde scurried beneath the covers to hide.

"Can I make some coffee at least?"

"No time, you gotta get out there now. It's a real mess!"

"Damn, kid. Well, let me get some pants on."

"Yes, sir." The young man remained in the doorway, panting and pretending not to stare at the soft girl's figure peeking out of the rumpled covers.

"That means git out!" William reached down retrieving a boot from next to the bed and hurled it at Jonah's head.

Jonah ducked, "Sorry," he said, fumbling to shut the door behind him while sneaking one last glimpse.

William looked down at his dimple-cheeked companion. "Sorry, darlin'. I gotta go."

She smiled and pressed her body to his, "It's too early. Stay a little longer."

"Can't. Gotta see what's got everyone so lathered up. Besides, you best git on home. I'm sure your ma must be wondering where you got off to last night."

"Let her wonder." The girl squinted her face with a mischievous glow and gave a playful nip to his bare shoulder. "You sure you can't stay for just a bit more?" She purred into his ear.

"That's enough of that." He gave the girl a gentle pat to her bare bottom and rolled out of the small bed.

Chapter 5 — The Ride out to the Black Cross Ranch

William dressed and shooed his bedmate out the door while Jonah procured a thermos of burnt coffee and a pouch of jerky from the restaurant and mercantile. He came back with the supplies as well as his own horse and he and the sheriff rode away for the Black Cross Ranch.

"Where we going anyway?" William asked.

"Out past Red Bluff Landing."

"Damn, Jonah. That's half a day's ride! Why is this such an emergency? If there was a fire out there, there's nothing I can do for them now."

"Graham needs you, is all."

"This is bullshit, kid."

"Don't I know it! I've been up dealing with this since the middle of the night."

"So, what is it they need me for anyway?"

"You'll see."

They rode hard for the next three hours, stopping to water and rest their horses occasionally. By noon, the sun pounded down on them and they were coated in a thin paste of sweat and dirt. They came over the rise at Red Bluff Landing and looked down into the stark valley.

An ink-black cloud rose up. The oily smoke tickled their nostrils as it spread out and up from the Black Cross Ranch. William had expected to see livestock or well-tended fields. All he saw was dry earth, boulders, and the charred remains of a large farm complex as they approached.

"What do they raise out here?" he asked.

"Mostly we don't ask."

William grimaced at Jonah's lack of information. They slowed and let the steeds trot the last quarter mile. Their animals snorted and twitched as they entered the property.

William had figured there might be some unpleasantness. The overnight barbecue of the ranch's inhabitants had coated the surrounding atmosphere with the charred stench of death. He fought back the churning in his stomach. It was probably best he didn't have time for a full breakfast before hitting the trail, besides the salty jerky and stale coffee he had choked down during their ride.

"William, over here!" the mayor of Thrall said, waving in the approaching sheriff and Jonah from a spot near a smoldering barn.

"Graham," William said. He swallowed back the rising bile and dismounted his nervous horse.

"William. I'm glad you came."

"It is my job, ain't it? Now what the hell happened?"

"Not exactly sure. I just know Hank, the ranch hand

from the Triple G just over the ridge, was out just past dusk last night gatherin' up stray sheep when he came over the hill and saw this place lighting up the valley. He rode straight into town and got me."

"Why did he go for you and not me?"

"This particular ranch is a bit of a delicate matter." Graham shifted, growing visibly uncomfortable.

"Delicate matter? So, who lived here that I was not privy to?"

"Someone with money and a penchant for privacy."

"Privacy?"

"Yep." Graham tightened up, avoiding William's inquisitive gaze.

William looked around, perplexed by Graham's reasoning. "If the owners were in there when it went up, they ain't there no more. That means there is nothing for me to do here except puke my guts out and go home."

"They were inside, but not all of them are quite gone yet."

"How's that?"

Graham motioned for William to follow. Jonah stood with the horses as they headed towards the smoldering barn that crackled under the noon sun. There was another sound bubbling beneath the crunching of their footsteps that peeked out from the wreckage like a soft moaning wind on a stormy night.

"What the hell, Graham? Are you saying that someone is in there?" William's pace quickened, hastening towards the pained moans.

"Wait, William..."

Chapter 6 - In the Barn

The charred door dangled from the blackened skeletal frame of the barn. William didn't break stride as he kicked through its burnt remains. He skidded to a halt, seeing the horror inside the decimated structure.

A mass of bodies huddled together in the shaded corner of a horse stall. Their blackened skin was peeling away, exposing the glutinous pink sinew beneath. They were a pulsing atrocity that stank of death.

"What the..." William gasped. His veins throbbed with adrenaline as he stared into the sharp-toothed ghouls' milky eyes.

At first, he thought they were victims of the fire not yet resigned to the grave. But their eyes did not plead to be put down.

Graham approached him. "That is why we brought you out here."

"What are they?"

"Our constituents and the county's dark secret."

"I don't understand."

"You don't need to. All you need to know is that we have been afforded an opportunity to rid ourselves of a problem and it's your job to take care of this...Sheriff." Graham attempted to offer up an axe, but William ignored his gesture.

William struggled to argue as he wrestled with the horrific image. A whisper snaked its way through his thoughts. It was weak, but words and images, not his own, cleared in the swirling mist of his mind, solidifying with a single word:

"*Food!*"

He clutched his skull, almost floored by the deafening rumble behind his eyes.

"They're talking to you, aren't they?" Graham said, placing his hands on William's shoulders to steady the struggling sheriff. "You have to fight it. I wasn't strong enough to do this, but you are."

Opalescent eyes bore into William as he fought the repeating word growing in intensity in his head.

"*FOOD!*"

"You have to finish them, William. You have to fight through the pain for the sake of all of us."

William dropped to his knees pressing palms to ears as if to shield him from the deafening shouts that clawed at his brain.

"Get up, William! They're healing and if you don't kill them, we're all dead," Graham shouted as he pushed William to action. He held out the axe, but William continued to ignore him.

Tears streamed down William's face from the

mounting pressure in his skull. He shook his head and reached for his revolver. He felt as if he was lifting a fifty-pound weight. He squinted through his foggy, damp vision and leveled his gun on the charred figure that rose up from the ghoulish mound.

"*CLOSER!*"

He pulled back the hammer.

"*COME CLOSER!*"

He fired. His bullet tore through the figure.

"*YOU FOOL!*"

The creature didn't drop. The fresh wound closed. The surrounding tissue oozed into the empty space his bullet had created, fusing with the charred flesh that a moment ago had been flaking off in gooey clumps.

"No!" William screamed.

He didn't believe what he saw. He fired again and again and again. Tattered flesh speckled the wall behind the healing figures. They reacted to each concussive shot, but did not die.

"You have to take their heads, William." Graham tossed his axe at William's feet. "You have to destroy their heads!" He pointed to the discolored axe between William and the squirming mound of naked figures that grew more animated with every passing moment. They were healing. Their skin shifted from charred, to gray, to light pink as William hesitated.

At last, William dropped his gun and sprinted toward the mound. He scooped up the axe and drove towards the monsters that slithered in the shade.

"*WE WILL FEAST ON YOUR SOUL!*" The telepathic shouts reverberated between his ears as the creatures acted and spoke as one.

As he ran, his weapon raised, his primal scream drowned out their hisses and protests.

He brought the axe down between the center creature's milky eyes, splitting its skull and lodging it in the monster's spine. A hiss rang out from the slithering mass. William yanked the axe free and began to swing through neck after neck. The dull thuds from the execution continued as William's frantic hacking minced the bodies into slippery mush. Blood and viscera dripped from the blade, the handle, the walls, and coated William's face and body in sticky residue.

William swung until movement from the mound halted and the venomous shouting that echoed in his ears stopped. He could hardly lift the axe as he stood there, sobbing. Graham placed a hand on his blood-soaked shoulder.

William looked into Graham's eyes. Graham stared back with sad relief. William let go of the axe and Graham took it. Graham gave another squeeze to his shoulder, turned and walked away.

William dropped to his knees. The bloody mass of indistinguishable body parts pooled around him. His body shook as he wept.

Jonah walked up to William, a tin of kerosene sloshing at his side. "Graham says we need to finish what was started last night. Just to make sure."

William looked up into Jonah's dark eyes. He stood, took the canister and slapped the boy. Jonah staggered back, his cheek stained with the sheriff's massacre. He splashed the sharp-smelling accelerant across the bloody scene.

He turned to Jonah. "Get out," he said. He retrieved a single match from inside his jacket. He lit it off his chin stubble and flicked it through the air. The kerosene fumes ignited with a flash. He turned and walked out of the burning structure.

Outside, the three watched the blaze until it was a smoldering heap, then mounted their horses for the somber ride back to Thrall.

Chapter 7 - The Dark Ride Home

The unsettling jostle from the ride and the grip of adrenaline letting go made William keenly aware of the churning in his stomach. He leaned to the side and vomited the sour remains of coffee and jerky he had eaten on the earlier ride. Jonah, worried about the quiet cloud that had settled over William since the ranch, was ready with a tin flask of whiskey. He trotted up next to him and offered up the medicinal burn of rye to cleanse the sick from his mouth. William drank, swished, spat and drank again. He didn't drink to quench his thirst but to wash away the macabre scene that played over and over in his head.

Graham maneuvered his horse up next to William. "Take it easy. It's a long ride home."

William took a hard pull from the flask. "You should have told me."

"And what would I have told you that wouldn't have sent you out there before this to try and rid us of such abominations?"

"You hired me to protect the town and yet you kept this from me?"

"You were hired to appease the town and bring in settlers."

"What?"

"You didn't know the law when you were hired. You barely know the law now, but you keep the peace and your reputation helps the townsfolk feel secure. Today you just had to actually get involved in the dirty side of your job, Sheriff."

William thought for a moment, the rhymic bounce from his horse's trot ushered in the warm buzz of the whiskey. "You're a real ass." He took a swig, letting the burn of the alcohol sting his tongue. "*Mayor.*"

William gave his horse a kick with his heel, taking the gentle trot to a short gallop to put some distance between him and the other two.

He drank the flask empty on the way back to Thrall. The sun waned and the bright sky shifted toward dusk as the woozy comfort of inebriation settled over him. He came to the livery at the edge of town, shakily dismounted, and put his horse away for the night. He stumbled out the door of the barn and squinted into the glaring rays of the setting sun.

His vision was blurred from the whiskey, but he made out the lanky shadow of a dark figure just off to his left, leaning in wait against the wooden frame of the stable. Startled, he fumbled for his pistol on his hip. He wiped at his eyes with the back of his other hand to get a better look at the person straightening themselves and moving closer in the shadows. Visions of the mound of hissing flesh from earlier flashed across William's thoughts. He had to tell himself that he was just seeing a man. As the figure came in sight, he took notice that it wasn't a man, but a tall, thin boy wearing ill-fitting hand-me-downs and a too-big hat. The boy took a confident stance between William and the barn, his hand held at the ready above the heavy-looking six-shooter weighing down his belt.

William cleared his throat. "Who's there? What do you want?" He continued to back away to get the sun out of his eyes so he could focus on what was happening.

"I'm here to take you out, mister," the boy said, his voice breaking with pubescent charm.

"Go home, son. There ain't no fight for you here."

"Didn't ask to fight. I'm tellin' ya to draw, coward!"

"Don't do this, boy." William fought to reconcile his blurry vision that had conjured multiple figures in front of him.

"I'm no boy and I'm gonna prove it. Now, git ready, old man!"

"I said no!" William turned to go back into the barn.

"Don't you walk away from me!" The boy drew.

William recognized the sharp click of the hammer being pulled back on the skinny boy's six-shooter. William drew in a fluid action built on years of muscle memory and instinct.

The thunder from William's lonely bullet howled through the dusk, echoed by the empty click of the boy's unloaded pistol. The world turned slowly and even in William's inebriated haze he knew what had happened. The boy's pa had left the gun unloaded, but he was not experienced enough to feel the subtle difference between a loaded gun and an unloaded one. By contrast, William's drunken shot, meant to just wing the boy in the shoulder, had fallen short of its target and pierced the kid's heart.

The boy dabbed at the warm wet hole in his chest with disbelief. He looked up, gave a confused chuckle, then the life left his eyes and he dropped to the dust.

William dropped his gun and ran to the dead boy who the townsfolk would later confirm was Jesse. He would not get to know Jesse in his natural lifetime, but grew to know the nightly routine the boy's ghost would thrust him into over the coming years.

Chapter 8 — William's Walk, Part Two

William took his familiar place in front of the barn. A light breeze swirled around him. In the background, gunfire could be heard, but not by William. Only Jesse's raspy taunts held his attention.

"I'm here to take you out, mister." The wispy figure shimmered in the moonlight.

"I'm not in the mood for you tonight, Jesse."

"Didn't ask to fight. I'm tellin' ya to draw, coward!"

"How long we gonna keep doin' this kid?"

"I'm no boy and I'm gonna prove it. Now git ready, old man."

"Why can't you just let this go?"

"Don't you walk away from me!"

Jesse's apparition drew for the empty gun. With the same swiftness and instinct, William drew and fired, blasting another hole into the barn, pockmarked with years of duels between the taunting phantom and the embattled, aging gunslinger.

William's once steady hand shook. Night after night, Jesse called him out. His compulsion drove him to drop everything. Time stopped for him until his trigger was pulled. Jesse would repeat his lines on a loop until the events played out, holding William in their fateful moment, cemented to the ground. Resisting was futile, and Jesse didn't let him leave until their tragic play had run its course.

William holstered his heavy gun as Jonah, in his midthirties now but still the town's unofficial messenger, jogged up behind him in the moonlight.

"Sheriff, Sheriff!"

"What is it?" He dabbed the cold sweat from his brow on his jacket sleeve.

"There's been a fight at the Braided Pony! I've never seen nothing like it."

"All right. Run ahead and tell Earl I'll be right there."

Jonah nodded and spun, trailed by a plume of dust as he ran back to the Braided Pony.

A cold breeze teased William's ear. "See you tomorrow, Sheriff."

William brushed a single tear from his cheek, coughed his body back to life and headed off to deal with the happenings at the Braided Pony.

Chapter 9 — A Bargain Struck

William looked around the dusty room at the three dead bodies. Even for the Braided Pony, this was above and beyond the usual carnage. No one else seemed hurt and most of the regular activity had resumed with everyone steering clear of the pools of blood so as not to dirty up their boots.

He had gathered a few accounts of the scene from the regulars before entering. Their absurd stories conjured images that hadn't haunted him in a long time. They spoke of how quick all the men moved, and their exaggerated physical features that many called animal-like. After a couple of people mentioned the glint of fangs or pitch-black eyes, he assured them they had just had a bit too much to drink. But in the back of his mind, he saw the wriggling mound of hissing horror that he had dispatched so many years ago at the Black Cross Ranch. He waved off their narratives and decided to see for himself.

He made mental notes of the dead starting with the headless torso. The wound was consistent with a close-range shotgun blast. The body looked mostly untouched except for the glisten of blood specked down its front. He scanned up past the shoulders. The head had been replaced with the chaotic splatter of blood, brain, and tufts of hair that spread outward from the point of impact. He turned his attention to the second body.

The visual of the table leg protruding from the dead man's chest was jarring. He paced around the body, taking in the sight from all angles. He pondered the power necessary to stab a man through the rib cage, let alone what it would have taken to impale him on the dull table leg. Few men he had met over the years could pull off such a task. He shook his head in disbelief, turned and strode towards the third corpse at the foot of the bar.

William knelt down next to the lifeless body. He marveled at the craftsmanship of the wooden blade protruding out from the dead man's chest. He grabbed the handle and wriggled the blade free of its resting place. He examined it. He wiped it clean on the man's duster and stood to face Earl, who was already pouring a glass of whiskey for the sheriff. William's usual drunken haze had lifted some with the evening's activities, so the whiskey was a welcome gesture to soothe his frayed nerves before questioning the stranger.

William took a swig of whiskey. The cleansing elixir tamped down his unease and the unsettling visions that tugged at his nerves. The memories of the Black Cross Ranch hadn't assaulted him in a long time. He refused to believe that something like that was happening again. He looked at the stranger and gently exhaled the heat from the whiskey.

The stranger appeared at ease as he quietly sipped his drink. William wondered how a man could be so calm after a fight like that. There weren't any latent tremors from the rush of adrenaline, no darting eye of paranoia, just the picture of a man quietly sipping on his whiskey in the shadows.

William looked down at the blade he had pulled out of the dead man at his feet, then to the stranger, then to Earl.

There was room in his jail if he felt the need to lock up the stranger, but he wasn't sure he wanted someone capable of all this carnage taking up space in his town for any longer than necessary. As was already demonstrated, trouble followed this man, so the quicker he was gone the better.

"Whatcha wanna do, Sheriff?" Earl asked, refilling William's glass.

"I wanna get drunk, but it looks like that will have to wait for a bit." William focused on the shadowed table where the stranger sat.

"Really?" Earl eagerly made to retrieve the shot glass before he gave up more free booze to the sheriff.

William placed a hand on his glass. "Slow down there, Earl. I've got some questions for our new friend and I ain't gonna ask them with a dry throat."

Earl smirked and filled the glass to the brim. "You got it."

William threw down the harsh liquid in a single swallow. He signaled Earl to fill it again. He begrudgingly did, and William took up the glass and joined the stranger.

"You interested in giving your side of the story, mister?" William asked, chasing his question with a small sip from his glass.

"I am if you're interested in hearing it."

"Indeed I am. Why don't we start with what I should call you?"

"Name's Finn." The hard-featured man pushed the chair across from him out with his foot.

William eased his tired body into the chair, took another sip of his whiskey and gestured for Finn to begin.

"Let's just say, me and the unfortunate fellow over there," Finn gestured towards the body at the bar, "been gunnin' for each other for quite some time."

"I know I'm just a local lawman, but I need more than that to put this to bed without going through the trouble of locking you in my jail tonight."

"He was kinda like an uncle."

"So, it's a family feud then?"

"You could say that."

"But would you say that?"

"Yeah, it's a family thing," Finn said. "He figured I did him wrong a few years back, and I figured he was dead already, so I didn't need to worry about running into him anymore."

"You saying that all this is over, then? 'Cause honestly, I should lock you up and wire for a judge to settle all of this." William watched for Finn's reaction, but Finn didn't even twitch.

"You do what you think you need to do, but I'm not a

fan of cages." Finn's tone was even and calm.

They continued sizing each other up while their glasses emptied and filled and emptied and filled. William was ready to wrap up the conversation, but was still concerned about the scene described by some of the folks he had questioned. There had to be some sort of explanation for the fangs and claws comments.

"Tell you what. If you can explain a couple of things, we will call it what you say...a family feud that boiled over in the bar. Ok by you?"

"I'll do my best. What's gnawing on ya, Sheriff?"

"What's this nonsense about these fellas sprouting fangs and claws and getting all weird-looking during your fight?"

Finn frowned. "Well, I can't speak for them," he gestured around the room to the dead men, "but if you take a quick look at my smile, you will see a couple of sharp teeth in there." Finn turned to William and flashed large white teeth. His canines did appear to be just a bit longer than the rest and came to rounded points.

"Yep, I see that." William said.

"These run in my family. Believe it or not, my ma had a pair of fangs that poked through her closed mouth, even. Nothing nefarious, just elongated canines that have been in my family for generations." Finn turned back to face the room and took another drink.

The story didn't matter much to William. He wanted to gauge Finn's reactions and body language to see how full of shit he was. He decided he was no more than any other drifter who had gotten caught up in trouble. It was not going to be worth the hassle of locking him up. He didn't need a judge to tell him what to do. He just needed the trouble to move on.

"You plan on causing any more trouble while you're in my town?" He said.

"I don't even plan on hurting a fly while I'm here. All I was looking for was a drink, a bath, and a bed." Finn filled William's empty glass. "Maybe solicit some companionship."

"Well, I can't say I could encourage our fine ladies to entertain such a violent character as yourself, but their livelihood is their business, I guess."

"Much obliged for your understanding."

"Honestly, I didn't know these men you've killed and I don't know you. I'm not one to buy into superstition and outlandish tales of monsters, so as far as I'm concerned, as long as the mess is paid for, then we are done here."

William placed the wooden blade on the table and slid it towards Finn. Finn nodded and replaced it to the sheath on his hip. He raised his glass to the sheriff. They emptied their drinks in unison.

"One more?" Finn offered up the bottle of rye to refill the sheriff's empty glass.

"One more."

Finn filled the glasses and the two sat quietly for a few minutes as they drained their drinks.

"I would appreciate if you could be on your way tomorrow. I hope you understand."

Finn nodded. "I understand and will be on the road first thing. I just have to resupply, and I will be on my way."

William pushed back in his chair and stood up, still

cradling his empty glass. "I hope this will be our last conversation."

Finn looked up from under his wide brim. "Yes, sir." His hard silver eyes assured William that his word was good.

William tipped his hat. He turned and headed out, halting at the swinging doors. "Earl, make sure our friend compensates you for the damages and the cleaning. He'll only be here for the night, so make sure he is taken care of as long as his gold is good."

Earl nodded and William disappeared into the quiet dark.

Chapter 10 – Ruby Makes Her Play

The saloon was restored to its natural clutter. Only the scuff marks from dragging the bodies away and the air-drying splotches from frantically mopping up the first man's lost head remained as evidence of the brawl.

Drink in hand, Ruby turned towards the stranger. Their eyes met and Ruby made her move on him. Smile wide, hips swinging, soft curves bouncing, she headed for the man's table.

"You looking for a friendly face to share the evening with, stranger?" She asked.

"The chair is open, ma'am. You're welcome to rest your feet for a while."

"That's mighty gentlemanly of you, sweetie." She rounded the front of the chair and took a seat next to him. She tipped her glass in a motion of cheers and slugged it back.

Ruby looked at him, a glint of mischief in her eye. "My name's Ruby. What's yours?"

"Name's Finn."

"So, Finn, what brings you to our corner of the world?"

"Looked cozy."

Ruby laughed. "A lot of things we are, but cozy ain't one of em."

"Depends on your definition."

"So what's yours?"

"A bath, a bed, and a bottle of whiskey."

"One outta three so far." Ruby pointed to the bottle.

"I was hopin' to be three for three before the night was up."

"Well, I can certainly help you out with the last two, but it'll cost you."

"Not worried about money, just the company."

"Don't worry, honey. I don't bite. Unless you want me to." Ruby winked.

"Yeah. But I might."

Ruby giggled and squinted into the silver pools of Finn's eyes. She swore he hadn't blinked once since she sat down.

"Earl." Ruby called over her shoulder. "When Roy finishes up with his errand, tell him to fill my bath with fresh hot water, would ya?"

"You sure about that, Ruby?" Earl said. An uneasy glance at Finn.

"Earl, you know I can take care of myself."

She turned back to Finn. "It will be about an hour before everything is set for you. So you just take your time with the rest of that bottle and then come on up to my room."

Finn dipped his hat forward.

Ruby smiled, gave him a wink and an inviting squeeze to his forearm. She pushed off and skipped up the stairs to her room to prepare for company.

Chapter 11 - The Evil Beneath

Candles and rose water wafted from Ruby's room as Finn opened her door. His duster trailed like a grand cape, his saddle bags strewn over one shoulder, and his spurs jingled as he strode in. Ruby closed the door behind him and turned the key with a heavy clunk, ensuring they would not be disturbed.

Ruby's accommodations hummed with femininity. Delicate patterned silks lay across chairs and covered windows. Candelabras burned and her bed rolled with blankets, velvet pillows, and a crimson-and-black patterned bedcover. An ornate, three-paneled changing screen was tucked into the corner, out of sight of any windows that overlooked the street. Next to the shimmering screen, steam rose from the large copper basin of fresh bathwater.

Finn surveyed the room, plotting every angle and exit point. No traces of anyone hidden away, waiting to rob him. No unwanted eyes on the landing outside the window looking to steal a peep.

He smiled at the soft nature of the decor and walked toward the basin. He set his bags down and breathed in the floral scent that infused Ruby's den.

"If you're shy, I can step outside while you get your bath," Ruby said. "Granted, nothing you got that I haven't seen before, but some men are more delicate than others when it comes to revealing themselves to a lady."

"I'm not shy. Just don't want to make you blush is all." Finn said and turned to reveal a playful smile.

"A bit feistier than you were downstairs. I like that."

Finn pulled away the shroud of his hat and his dark, wavy locks fell across his shoulders. He took his duster off and laid it flat across the lap of a chair, then settled his hat atop the cushioned headrest.

He sat and reached down to free his tired feet from his boots. Ruby went down on one knee to assist. Finn leaned back and worked his foot loose. The boot gave way and Ruby tumbled backward, landing with a thump. She looked up at Finn and giggled. The second boot came free with ease and Ruby gathered the worn footwear up and set them next to his saddlebags.

Finn gazed into Ruby's eyes and cradled her chin in his hand.

"That's enough of that." she said. "Now git in that tub. You may look fancy in this candlelight, but you don't smell like Prince Charming."

Finn grinned, stood and shed the remainder of his soiled clothing. He entered the tub with a slosh. He sat down and stretched out his lean frame, lounging against the smooth walls of the wash basin. He exhaled his tension and closed his eyes. A minute later, he opened them to see Ruby's soft foot curve its way down into the water.

"I don't get fresh baths that often, so I might as well take advantage of it—along with the company," she said, as her smooth, naked curves lowered down into the hot water, rubbing up against his chest as she situated between his legs, leaning back on him like a fur-covered, well-muscled chair.

"Far be it from me to argue with a lady," Finn said, his lips brushing across the back of her ear.

The two giggled and bathed and writhed together in the tub until the heat had gone and they were left grappling to each other for warmth in the sudsy remains. Ruby snuggled with her cheek on his chest, both of them breathing hard from their romp.

"You're fun, mister." She gave Finn a squeeze and raised herself from the tub. Finn gave her a playful pat on her wet buttocks as she stepped out onto the floor. She retrieved a silk robe from behind the changing screen. When she came back, Finn gazed hungrily at the damp robe clinging to her wet figure.

"I knew there was something about you when you strolled in tonight," Ruby said, settling at her vanity to brush out her wet hair.

Finn stepped out of the tepid bathwater. "Yeah, what's that?" He retrieved a towel and dried himself.

"It's the way your kind moves, fights, even loves. You offer me what no other man can."

"My kind? I've had women call me an animal before, but-—" Finn nervously smiled at Ruby in the mirror. She smiled back.

She turned and the soft features that were present during their love-making sharpened. Her almond-shaped eyes darkened. "Yes," her smile widened as she spoke. "A creature that is fierce, lightning-fast, and feeds on the death of those around him."

Finn's face paled. "Darlin', you feeling okay? You're not looking right." He said as he edged towards the door.

Ruby sprang up and was on him before he could react. His heightened strength and speed were useless against her as she clamped her iron grip around his wrists and they toppled to the ground. Stricken with panic, Finn struggled for freedom.

Ruby stared down at him with ravenous glee. She dug deep into his arms and pumped her paralytic poison into him. He couldn't move or yell and he could barely breathe as her venom took hold.

"You don't know, do you?" Ruby's voice rattled in the back of her throat. "Every soul you take leaves a residue behind. A little piece of them that hangs on you. It colors your shadow and flavors your flesh. It fates you for my kill. It sweetens your death so that I can bathe in the essence of a hundred lives as I drain you of yours." She wet her lips. "I will lick the last drops of them from your teeth as I devour you. I only wish you had not dispatched your friends so quickly. You robbed me of quite the feast. I will just have to settle for you."

Her smirk widened to a horrific gash, revealing a cavernous maw riddled with jagged, translucent fangs. She loomed over Finn. Saliva and tattered membrane congealed, dropping away in sloppy wads on Finn's chest.

Her sour breath scratched at his nostrils as she lapped the fear-stained sweat on his skin.

Ruby's continuous infusion of poison magnified his pain and fear receptors so that even in his benign state he was hyper-aware. He wanted to give up and float away, but he was jailed inside the augmented experience of being dinner. He realized he was no longer the killer that grown men feared and that mothers spoke of in hushed voices as the soul-stealing terror in the dark. Now he was the prey! Finn's horror seasoned his flesh for Ruby's rapturous consumption.

Her tongue writhed with feral abandon, painting the air with viscous drool. It whipped the air, swiping razor-fine cuts on his chest, sampling the goods before the meal. Droplets of blood raced from his wounds and were lapped up before they hit the floor.

"That's right. Try and scream for me, baby." Her thoughts echoed in his head, telepathically taunting him.

Her bulbous eyes rolled back with the ecstasy of the feeding. Her mouth gaped wide. She arched back and pounced down into his chest. The jagged teeth tore into his flesh, coating the roof of her mouth in his metallic ooze. She propped his hands behind his head, elevating his gaze, forcing him to view the excavation site where she tore past cartilage and bone, boring her tongue further into his body, searching for her ultimate prize—his beating heart.

Finn felt every tooth burrow into his rib cage, cutting, breaking and tearing away the protective layer of bone. His internal screams reverberated in Ruby's skull, growing in pitch and intensity as her feeding continued.

The crunch of ribs rupturing drowned out his psychic howls. She tore the rib cage loose, dripping carnage down her chin. Her taut breasts shone through her blood-soaked robe, speckled with the tiny shards of bone escaping between the gaps in her teeth. She reached up and pulled the rib cage from her mouth, revealing the glistening underside. She lapped at the gore from the membrane clinging to the bones and cartilage.

Finn's chest plate thumped to the ground. A shudder ran through her. With every drop of blood, every crunch of bone, every explosion of crushed cartilage, her ecstasy grew. She rode the dying man with voracious glee. The screams in his head fueled her. His blood splashing down her throat was a series of exploding charges that heightened her pleasure.

She looked down into Finn's horror-stricken eyes. "This has been fun, lover, but it's time for me to be moving on."

Ruby released his arms and drove her talons deep into Finn's skull. She leaned down. Her tongue writhed and snaked into his chest, wrapping around his heart. She pulled away, tearing the connecting blood vessels and ventricles. She wrenched Finn's head off. The sound of muscles and tendons tearing rang in his ears as they stretched beyond their means. Bones crunched as they were pulled away from their host. Finn's psychic screams halted abruptly as his head tore loose and his heart was ripped from its nest. It beat three last pulses as Ruby displayed it in front of the twitching eyes of Finn's liberated cranium.

Ruby brought the heart into her mouth, savoring the

last moments of her kill. She clamped down and swallowed it in one euphoric gulp, letting the rapture roll through her, holding tight to Finn's head, his lower lip quivering spastically. She loosened the claws from one hand, letting the head gently swing by her side. Her face returned to its human shape and she smiled at her bloody features in the vanity mirror.

She took the rest of the night to tidy up. She washed away the remnants of Finn that clung to her and burned her clothes, all under Finn's watchful dead eyes. She excavated his teeth and dropped them into a leather pouch. A gentle tinkle rang forth as the ivory trophies clattered against the other teeth.

Ruby's victims were not a daily convenience. She would have to await another of his kind before she could be satiated again. Until then, she would have the residue of the countless souls encrusted on those procured teeth to flavor her daily tea. The key to her sultry facade and the strength that she needed to effectively take down her next unassuming victim.

Come morning, she would be cloaked in her new pale leather duster and matching Stetson, loaded down with her saddlebags filled with Finn's belongings and gold, in search of a new town, a new saloon, and new victims.

Chapter 12 — A Resurrection in the Dark

The back alleys of Thrall echoed with the noisy passage of Roy and Slim. Their wheelbarrow loaded down with the corpses from the Braided Pony ground along the rough path. They ricocheted against each other as they carted their heavy load off to the town burn pile.

Slim stomped on Roy's foot, "Ow! Watch it ya idiot!" Roy hollered.

"Watch it yourself. It's not my fault you keep g'tting' in my way." Slim shouldered his surly partner.

Roy shoved back, rocking the wheelbarrow off balance. Samuel's dead weight shifted and the two men yelped as the rickety cart's awkward trajectory keeled it to the side, dumping its cargo in the dust. Slim collided with the cart's handle, bruising his soft gut.

"Damnit, Roy!' He shouted and cradled his sore paunch.

Roy laughed at his fumbling partner. "Serves ya right. Pay attention next time."

Slim retorted with a meaty fist to Roy's mouth, loosening two of his last six rotten teeth.

"You payin' attention now?"

Roy bent over, holding his mouth and capturing the fresh pool of fluid that surfaced from his loosened teeth. He pulled his hand away to survey the stream of blood dripping into his hand.

"You broke my teeth, you ass!"

"How can you tell? You can't even count the few that you have, you diseased donkey."

Roy fumed as Slim laughed at him. He charged Slim, his face red and swollen with anger, a slight trail of red streaming off his chin. He tackled Slim and the two men tussled in the dirt.

Blood flew from his fingers. The droplets plopped onto Samuel's hollow cheeks. As quickly as the droplets landed they disappeared, absorbed into his soulless body.

The old vampire's shriveled heart bounced to life with the scant infusion of nutrients. Samuel's dead eyes flew open. He scanned left to right and left again, hunting for the source of the blood that had shocked him back to consciousness.

Embroiled in their exchange of half-hearted blows, Roy and Slim didn't notice Samuel rise up above their bumbling skirmish. Samuel licked his lips, hungry for the wet meal that coursed through the bodies grappling on the ground. The few drops he absorbed fired up his aged husk, but he required more fuel to recover from his battle with Finn.

A low rumbling growl rose from Samuel's gut, overpowering the sounds of the scuffle. He stared down at the two combatants, deciding which to quench his thirst with. He didn't care which one ended up at the other end of his primal bite. He drove his talon-engorged hand into the flailing mound. The elongated claws tore through fabric and flesh and he clamped down into the back of the first figure that rolled into his grip. The two men fought each other for another couple seconds until Slim realized it was not Roy that was stabbing him. Samuel lifted him up by the clumped fat on his back. Slim went from punching his friend to clawing to keep hold of his sparring partner.

Slim screamed for Roy to help, but Roy was caught up in the skirmish. He swung upward, popping Slim in the jaw, stunning him. In the second of quiet, Roy gathered his thoughts. He squinted through the dust in search of Slim who was now hoisted above him. A good six inches separated Slim's toes from the dusty earth and his scuffle with Roy had been replaced by the wrestle for his own life with the beast that held him captive. He kicked and screamed as Samuel's talons sank into his flesh.

Samuel worked fast. He bared his fangs and drove the saliva-lubricated daggers into Slim's salty flesh. Slim fought, but to no avail. Samuel sucked the blood reserves from his heart, quenching the dry thirst of death.

Roy froze with horror. His mouth gaped as he watched Slim's fruitless struggles. Samuel's distended stomach stretched outward as the final remnants of Slim's life drizzled down his throat.

Samuel pulled away. A sticky mesh of skin, saliva, and blood tethered his mouth to the open wound on Slim's neck. Roy gawked at the macabre ventriloquist vision looming over him. Samuel loosened his grip and Slim's lifeless husk flopped to the ground. Samuel had left nothing except Roy's memories of his dead friend.

Samuel sighed. His thirst was quenched and the warmth of life gushed through his veins. He turned his thin, graceful hands around in the dancing firelight. Painted in the sticky hue of Slim, they shimmered in the pop and crackle of the bonfire. His crimson talons retreated to the less aggressive and rounded appearance of a high-dollar show girl. He caught Roy's horrified gaze, winked and lapped at the sticky remnants that lingered on his hand and under his nails. He groomed away the remaining droplets until there was no further evidence of his feeding.

Roy sat in the acrid stench of his own fear, having soiled himself. Samuel's expression softened. He took a step towards Roy, hid a quiet burp, exhaling Roy's friend, then asked, "So my friend. Are you a meal, or can you prove yourself to be useful in other ways?" He sniffed at the air and held his nose. "That is, once you have properly bathed." Samuel grinned, a hint of pink coloring his lips and teeth.

Roy curled up in a fetal position and sobbed, repeating in a hiccupped and broken pattern. "Oth...er..wa..ayysss...oth...er...waa..aayyyss..."

"Good. Let's get to work then." Samuel chuckled and flung Slim's limp body onto the burn pile. The flames roared as Slim lit the night with his sacrifice.

Chapter 13 – A Rude Awakening

William's sparse quarters resonated with his whiskey-laced snores. He was startled from his drunken slumber by the small, breathless figure that burst through his door.

"Sheriff, Sheriff. We got a body!" Tim yelled, every other syllable punctuated by a gasp, panting hard from his run across the small town.

William shot up, immediately regretting it. He pushed back the oily film of bile that stung his throat. His pounding head did little to quell the urge to pull his revolver on the young intruder. He held a hand up, halting the boy's panicked shouts.

"Timmy, what the hell are you gettin' on about?" He swallowed back a rancid burp.

"Sorry, Sheriff. There's another body at the Braided Pony. Earl said to come get you right away." It was ten in the morning and way too early to deal with more carnage.

William held his throbbing head, soaking in the

consequences of his post-Braided Pony binge. He threw his covers off and flung his legs over the edge of his cot. The rickety contraption groaned with his shifting weight. He cleansed his pungent breath with the final remnants of backwash-laden whiskey from one of the teetering bottles that lined his bed.

"You okay, Sheriff? Should I run and tell 'im you're on your way?" The skinny boy fidgeted in the doorway.

"Sure, kid. Tell 'im I'll be there in a bit."

"Yes, sir."

"Hey, who's the unlucky soul?"

"It was the stranger." Tim turned tail and was gone.

William was dumbfounded. He had seen what Finn could do. The fact that he was dispatched without waking half the town in a barrage of violence didn't make sense.

The lingering drunkenness clung to him as he navigated his room. He hobbled over to his rusted wash basin. He waved off the loitering flies that hovered over the tepid water. He splashed cold water on himself. The chill tackled the haze from his hangover. He got dressed, slicked his hair back under his sweat-stained hat and slapped on his gun belt. He grabbed his worn leather jacket and was off to the Braided Pony once again, this time to investigate the death of his deceased drinking partner.

Chapter 14 – A Grisly Scene

"Sorry to bring you back so soon, Sheriff," Earl said on the main floor of the saloon, his chin glistening from dabbing what looked like puke from his chin.

"No worries, Earl. What am I in for, anyway?" William reached into his jacket pocket to retrieve a roughly wrapped roll of chaw.

"It aint pretty, that's for sure."

"Is it just the stranger or do we have other bodies, too?"

"Don't think so. Looks like just him. But I didn't stick around to get a close look."

William plucked his chaw from its greasy wrapper. He took a healthy bite and secured it between his cheek.

"The stranger, huh? That don't track." He looked at Earl, who was swishing whiskey in his mouth.

"It may not track, but it's what I gathered from my quick look."

"Hmm."

"Have at it, Sheriff. Door's unlocked."

William turned to the staircase and headed for Ruby's room. Halfway up the stairs, he cocked his head over his shoulder and asked, "Where's Ruby, then?"

"Not sure. Haven't seen her since last night when she disappeared up to her room with him."

"Ain't that peculiar now." William continued up the stairs, stopping at the entrance. He examined the door and its frame for signs of forced entry. None.

William placed his hand on the doorknob, took a deep breath and exhaled. He eased the door open. The daylight peeking through the curtains reflected off the wet surfaces inside and painted the room a maroon hue.

He couldn't believe the gore all over the place. Blood pooled outward from the body near the bath basin. Splatter coated the furniture and walls. It dripped from the ceiling like stalactites, partially coagulated with a tempered sheen, having dried unevenly overnight. Interestingly, the bed was neatly made, even though it was streaked with drying blood.

William stood silent and motionless. He bit into the side of his cheek. The pain helped him focus.

He swished the blood, saliva, and tobacco juice around in his mouth. He spat into the corner behind the door, splattering Finn's insides with his own spittle.

"You okay, Sheriff?" Earl called up from the bar.

"Yeah. I'm okay." William wiped his chin clean.

He gulped. Time to inspect the body.

Blowflies crawled all over the remains of the man he had drunk whiskey with the night before. William stepped over the bloodstains covering the floor as well as he could and knelt next to the mangled, fly-ridden corpse.

While he examined it, Finn gazed down on him from where the head had been propped on the vanity. William turned away from the awful sight and examined the punctures on the arms. He poked and prodded the pale flesh with his hunting knife. He traced his blade around the space where Finn's chest used to be.

After he'd seen enough, he stood and went to the windows.

"I'm gonna open the curtains to get some light and fresh air in here, okay, Earl?" he shouted.

"Do whatcha gotta do, Sheriff."

William swept aside the curtain and flooded the nightmarish scene with morning sunlight. Finn's body sizzled and sparked. He closed the curtain and watched the body again. The tiny flames that had started went out.

Testing his sanity, William opened the curtain again. Flames rose wherever the sunlight landed. He had seen this before: That day at the Black Cross Ranch. The last day he felt a grasp on reality.

Footsteps sounded in the hall outside. William dropped the curtain as Earl burst into the room.

"What the hell are you doin' up here?" The bartender covered his mouth and coughed from the thick smoke filling the room.

William ran to the bed, whipped off the top cover and laid it on the smoking corpse.

"Sorry, Earl. Did you see that, though?" He coughed.

"I wish I hadn't. What is going on here?"

"I have no idea, but let's keep this body covered and

out of the light until sundown just in case we're both not crazy."

The two men patted away the last of the smoldering heat under the blanket.

"Earl, can you have your boys bundle this up and have it taken down to the ice house?"

"I'd say yes, but honestly, I haven't seen those two idiots since they finished cleaning up the mess from last night."

"What? Where'd they go?"

"Who knows. Sometimes it's a couple days till I see them if they get it in their head to go off on a bender, and after last night's clean up, I wouldn't blame em' for emptying the entire town of homemade hooch."

William spat on the floor.

"Okay. Help me cart this down there till I can get this figured out?"

"Yep. I'll round up another wheelbarrow at least so we don't have to try and walk this halfway across town on our shoulders. Wouldn't want it to catch fire on us, after all."

"All right, then," William said. "I'll roll this up into the rest of these covers while you do that."

The two men went to work. William didn't envy whoever would be tasked with the rest of the clean-up.

As they finished up in the room, he looked toward the bath basin. A shape caught his eye. He walked over and tapped his toe on the end of a sheath. He knelt down and picked up the blade Finn had used to dispatch the third fighter the night before. He pulled on the handle and the sheen of the wooden blade caught the light. He ran a finger across the edge, lifting a thin trail of blood from his finger. "Ow!" He sucked on the wound and looked in wonder at the finely hewn blade. He slid it back into the leather casing and slipped it onto his belt for safekeeping.

Chapter 15 — Ruby Makes Her Exit

Ruby rode away from Thrall clad in Finn's duster and hat to protect her from the ravages of the morning sun. Her allergic reaction to its rays took time to heal if she was exposed to it for too long. She was glad that Finn was so well outfitted.

She was also glad that his horse was conditioned not to fear Finn's kind and that it did not seem to mind her kind, either. Of course, it probably didn't hurt that she smelled of Finn.

As for the local authorities showing her any opposition, she knew the sheriff couldn't leave town for long because of his strange nightly ritual, walking through the streets drunk and shooting at the livery.

Rider and mount kept a steady pace throughout the day. Ruby would nod off and let the horse guide her to the next watering hole or river where they would rest and bed down. The horse would graze the night away while she lay under the stars reciting the songs of her ancient childhood and breathe in the crisp air of the wild.

The next town was only another day away. She had time to decide if she wanted to overtake an outlying farm for some peace and quiet or partake in another house of flesh to toy with the mortals that paid for her company. She would wait to see what the next town had in store.

Thrall had been one of her favorite way posts. So many strangers' depraved energy to satiate her cravings. She licked at the edge of her lips, tasting the recent memories that flooded her thoughts.

She continued on, entertained by her imagination until her horse chuffed, signaling the upcoming river. It was time to find a spot to rest as the sun rounded the sky and edged close to the rim of the surrounding hills. The shadows of the day stretched across the serene valley before them.

Chapter 16 — William Meets Samuel

William and Earl carted Finn's body down to the ice house. The smell of charred death awakened the memories William had worked to tamp down with years of whiskey. Flashes of blackened skin and screams of pain in the depths of a smoldering barn...

After sending Earl back to the Braided Pony to finish cleaning up, William plodded back to his cot. The day was sticky on his skin and he wanted nothing more than to fall into a bottle of booze and wash away the stench of death.

He rushed through the door of the jail, searching for the nearest bottle. They clattered as he kicked past the glass empties that littered the path to his footlocker. In his desperation, he didn't notice two figures watching him.

He threw open the chest at the foot of his bed and retrieved a pint-sized bottle of tea-colored hooch. He wrestled the cork free and spilled the antiseptic brew down his throat. He drank, coughed, spat, drank.

"Rough day at the office, Sheriff?"

William started at the smooth tenor voice. He dropped the bottle and drew his Colt. He saw a shadow in one corner and leveled his gun barrel at it with a shaky hand.

"Who's there?" He said, cocking the hammer back on his six-shooter.

"The bullets will hurt, but they won't do what you hope they will," the stranger said. "You might as well put the gun away so we can have a gentlemanly chat."

"I'm not in the mood to chat. So unless you wanna test your theory with my pistol you best git outta here. Or I guess I'll hafta drag another body down to the ice house."

"Is that where our friend Finn has been laid?" The stranger took a step forward into the dim candle light of the room.

"Not one more step. I'm warning you."

"There's no need for dramatics, Sheriff."

"I said no closer!"

The stranger halted. "So touchy today. Did you see something up there you were not expecting?"

"Why? What should I have expected?"

"You probably expected to see a girl up there dead from a passionate scuffle. What did you see instead?"

"I...I saw Finn's body torn open and his insides ripped out." He softened his grip on the trigger. "How did you know that it wasn't the girl?"

"Well, had it been the girl, you might've been shaken when you saw the scene, but not drown-yourself-in-rotgut shaken."

William released the mechanism holding back the gun's hammer but still kept the gun on the stranger as he paced back and forth.

"Who are you?" William asked.

"I'm someone who wants what you want."

"And what's that?"

"Justice and answers."

Then the man was nose-to-nose with William before the rush of wind even hit him. He directed William's gun hand off to the side.

William pulled the trigger. The bullet hit his desk.

"Jesus, Sheriff! Watch it." Roy came around from behind the desk.

"Shit!" Till that moment, William had not seen a third man in his office. "Roy, is that you?"

The stranger laughed. "Enough with the introductions. Would you mind putting the gun away so we can have a serious conversation?" He let William go as a show of good faith.

William holstered his weapon and shoved the man away. "Get outta my face, at least. I ain't paid for a kiss."

"Fair enough." The stranger took the chair behind the desk. William retrieved the half-empty bottle he had dropped. He took a swig.

"Now who in the name of all that's still holy in this world are you?"

"Well, I'm not holy. That's for sure." The stranger flashed sharpened canines in a playful, thin-lipped smile.

"I am not in the mood for cute."

William sat in the chair across from the stranger.

"Very well, Sheriff. At one point I was considered one

of your township's fine, upstanding tax payers. I owned a ranch just inside the county lines. You might have heard of it, in fact."

William took a stiff drink. "Which one?"

"Do you remember the Black Cross Ranch?"

William stopped in mid-swig and coughed violently. He dropped the bottle and the remaining backwash and liquor spilled down his chin. "What do you know about that place?"

"I know it was burnt to the ground. I know that many of my friends were lost in that fire. And I know that it was my old companion, Finn, who set the place alight that night."

"Those...things were your friends?" Williams' voice quivered.

"Careful, William. Don't judge too quickly the creatures under the skies of your God."

"Don't assume it is my God you speak of."

"Fair point. At any rate, it was you that put my friends out of their misery that morning, was it not?"

"Putting those things down was a service of mercy. Not for them, but for the world they were feeding on. If those things were your friends, then I stopped swinging my axe too soon."

"There is no need to be rude. I appreciate your swift action that day. They were in excruciating pain. But let's not be so rash. We can't all be created in the image of the higher being."

Sensing something ominous in the man's tone, William decided to change the subject. "Let's calm down. So last time I saw you, you were on the floor of the

Braided Pony in a much less lively state. You want to explain what the hell is going on?"

"I have a proposition for your tortured soul."

"I'm not in a habit of making deals with the devil."

"You flatter me Sheriff, but what if I could help you with your nightly walks?"

William blinked at the possibility of peace, even for a moment. "How did you—what are you suggesting?"

"I'm asking if you would like to free yourself from your evening torment."

"What do you know of that?"

"You stink of a kind of curse, William. It forces you night after night to relive that fateful encounter when you came back from the ranch. The gunfight that stole your taste for life."

The stranger stood and went to the box of bottles. "What if I could rescue you from your cycle of shame?" He selected the fullest one. The dirty brown liquid sloshed around as he held it to the lantern light to inspect it. He turned towards William. "What if I could break the shackles that bind you to that moment so many years ago?" He crossed the room, held out the bottle to William and flicked the cork from its mouth.

"What if you could?" William swiped the bottle from the man and took a healthy swig.

"Would that be worth enough to enlist your talents in a little adventure?"

"Adventure?"

"To free Finn from his captor."

"He's not a captive, he's fucking dead. I guarantee it."

"You guaranteed I was dead as well. Look how that

turned out."

William swallowed a large gulp and thought about the offer. Just the mention of his nightly sojourn to visit Jesse raised the hairs on the back of his neck.

"What exactly are you proposing?"

"Come along with us and I will rid you of your ghostly nuisance."

William let the words sink in as he drained another healthy dose of whiskey.

"Mister, let's say you ain't full o' shit. What's to say this is the only justice that poor boy has over me? Why would you rob him of his retribution?"

"Interesting questions, Sheriff. Who says the spirit haunting you is gaining any retribution? What if it is a mere echo of the boy that came to kill you that day? What justice is that if it is the both of you that are trapped in this hateful cycle?"

"How does that make any sense?"

"How does shooting holes in that barn every night just because some snot-nosed brat decided he was man enough to test his iron against you?"

"Tracks more than all the crazy shit that's happened in the past twenty-four hours."

"Well, this crazy shit is staring you in the face, unlike the transparent punk that haunts you every night."

William sat quiet for a moment. He drank and thought about a future without his nightly walk. He could once again eat dinner in peace, Entertain a soft scented woman. Travel beyond the reach of Thrall's borders. He could build a life beyond the dark barn he was shackled to.

"So what is your proposition?"

"I propose a partnership. I help you to sever the boy's hold on your soul. In exchange, you accompany us to get my old friend Finn back."

"What happens when you recover your friend?"

"He will face judgment for his actions at the Black Cross Ranch." The stranger paused to let William ponder and drink. "Well...what do you say, Sheriff?"

William thought for another moment, then finished off the bottle. "Break my hold with Jesse and this fucking town and I will go with you."

The man held out his hand. William grimaced at the gesture, but took the cold hand in his own.

The man squeezed tight and pulled William close to him.

"The name is Samuel," he said. He licked the tip of William's nose, then pushed him back into his chair, nearly toppling him backwards.

William steadied his chair and wiped the saliva off his face.

"God damn you," he said.

"Which one? Yours, this time?" Samuel smiled. "Now, let's get to work. Do you have anything of Jesse's that I can use?"

Chapter 17 – Preparations for the Untethering

"I feel like an idiot," William said.

"That must be a familiar feeling for you."

"Go to Hell."

William stood buck naked in front of his barn, Samuel behind him, spreading charcoal across his buttocks. The black runes marked his skin from head to toe. He frowned down at his and Jesse's guns that sat in a scribed circle in front of him, barrels crisscrossed.

"How much more of this shit do you gotta paint on me, anyway?"

"You don't think I'm touching your greasy ass for my own pleasure, do you?" Samuel gave a playful flick to William's butt cheek.

"That's enough!" William spun and cupped his genitals, concealing them from Samuel, Roy, and a woman passing by. "Ma'am," he said, performing a tip-of-the-hat gesture as she raised a hand to her mouth and hurried off.

Samuel chuckled. "I'm done. Now get back here and stand where I told you or this won't work." He pointed towards the design he had etched into the ground earlier.

William huffed and took his place for the ceremony. The cooling wind brushed his nakedness and mussed his hair as Samuel and Roy made final preparations.

That done, Samuel explained that Jesse was tied to the world because of the circumstances of his death. The soul couldn't let go of the perceived injustice of being killed in cold blood. The boy needed to win, but was held back by his own miscalculations on that fateful day. Hence both he and William were being punished for their parts in the boy's untimely death. The markings on William and their guns were spells to give the boy closure and sever his bond to the man who had killed him.

"So what's next?" William said.

"We wait for the boy to arrive."

After a few minutes, William felt the itch at the back of his brain that signaled the ghost's gradual emergence.

"He'll be coming soon, I figure."

"Okay. Now the hard part begins." Samuel knelt down and scrawled more etchings into the earth between the barn and William.

"What do I do now?"

"You lose."

Chapter 18 — Devil's in the Details

Frigid wind rolled through the haunted arena. Samuel stood beside William, mumbling incantations under his breath. William stood naked and shivering, his gut churning.

Out of habit, he felt for the guns that were not on his hips.

"Are you sure this will work?" He croaked.

"Be patient."

Samuel bent down to the dirt and scratched another series of symbols around the naked man. He looked up at William, his fangs showing. "Trust me."

William wanted to step back from the unnatural being, but realized he couldn't move.

"Hey, what's going on? I can't move!"

"You can't move because I can't have you screwing this up."

"I don't understand."

"No, you don't, which is why I have petrified you." Samuel stepped closer and cupped a soft, cold hand on

William's cheek. "The boy needs closure, right? And your soul — you might call it conscience — needs cleansing and sometimes the best way to do that is through the fire of death...or at least a perceived death. Spirits tend to be short-sighted and easy to fool."

"You mean you're going to trick Jesse into believing he shot me?"

"Sort of."

"But I still don't get how this is gonna work," William said, as Samuel walked away laughing. "Jesse never goes away until I fire my gun. I have stood here for hours just listening to him repeat his lines over and over until I finally pull the trigger."

"The words I have scrawled on you will help to break the cycle."

Minutes passed. William felt the tingle of Jesse's gradual emergence travel through his body.

"He's getting closer," he said.

"I know."

"But...something's wrong. I can't explain it, but I can feel it."

"Be patient. This will all be over soon."

Samuel began to recite incantations again.

Frozen to his spot, William listened to the unrecognizable language, to the wind, to the fear he couldn't describe.

"Hey...Samuel?"

Nothing.

"Samuel?"

Nothing again.

"Samuel, you son-of-a-bitch, you answer—"

A swirl of dust rose up in front of him. Jesse appeared in his usual place, ready to go through the motions.

Chapter 19 – The Untethering

"I'm here to take you out, mister."

The wispy figure shimmered in the moonlight.

William gulped. "Samuel, what do I do?"

The vampire's chanting grew louder.

"Didn't ask to fight. I'm tellin' ya to draw, coward!"

"Samuel, talk to me."

"I'm no boy and I'm gonna prove it. Now git ready, old man."

"Jesse, I hope you can hear me for once. We've already done this, kid."

"Don't you walk away from me!"

"Samuel, quit that babbling for a second. What do I do?"

The vampire continued to chant, the foreign words growing into a rumble. A wind blew through the area and howled around the barn.

"Samuel…?"

Samuel dropped to his knees, murmured another incantation, then fell silent.

Jesse's apparition drew for the gun. Feeling more naked than ever, William held his breath, terrified that it might actually be loaded thanks to Samuel's magic.

Click.

"What the..." The boy stared at his weapon, leveled it on William again and squeezed the trigger. *Click. Click.* "Well, shit," he said.

Then he noticed William watching him and looked him up and down. "Sheriff. Why you standin' there nekkid? I coulda sworn you had your clothes on a second ago." The confused boy lowered the heavy but useless metal in his hand to his side.

William turned to speak to Samuel and realized he could move again. "I'm free," he said. "Whatever you did, it worked!"

"Sheriff, what's goin' on?" Jesse worked the long barrel of the heavy cannon into his holster.

"I helped to sever your bond to this little scamp," Samuel said. "Isn't that what I was supposed to do?"

"Sheriff, what's going on and who is that guy next to you?"

"In a minute, Jesse. Okay, you've severed our bond, Samuel, but what does that mean, exactly? Is the kid still dead?"

"In a way. I snapped him out of his pattern."

"Wait, 'dead,'" Jesse cut in. "*Did you say 'dead?'*"

"Shut up, kid. Well, is he dead or isn't he, Samuel?"

"He is no longer tethered to you in the way he was before, making you available to accompany me on my journey, as we agreed."

"Dead..." Jesse murmured. "*Dead?*"

Chapter 20 – Jesse

As quickly as Jesse was ushered out of this world by William's bullet, his consciousness was snapped back by Samuel's incantation. Seeing the sheriff standing before him naked and covered in symbols came as quite a shock to him.

While the men argued, he took stock of his situation. He looked through his opaque extremities and noted the lack of his own shadow. The world used to have weight to it that he no longer felt. There was no gritty dirt grinding under his boot soles. His loose clothing lacked the sensation of cotton passing across skin. He was there, but not there.

He waved his hands in front of his face. The world shimmered through. Less so now that the sun was gone, and the shadows had melded together covering the town in a blanket of dusk. He definitely noticed less transparency the less light that shone around him.

The weight of his pa's heavy revolver was gone. The image of the sagging gun belt remained, but like his clothes, he didn't register the heft he remembered from what to him was mere seconds ago.

He noticed the breeze that wafted through the valley had no effect on him. He didn't feel the night's brisk chill. He couldn't smell the dry earth that blew around him. What was a world to him if there was no taste, no smell, no feeling? The questions filled his head and the only ones he felt could answer them were the naked sheriff and the odd-looking tall man that he was yelling at.

Chapter 21 – A New Life

"I thought you were going to get rid of him," William barked.

Samuel watched bemusedly as the sheriff nearly stumbled putting his pants on. "That's not quite how I remember our conversation," he said.

"Dead?" Jesse whimpered, inspecting his hands.

His dressing complete, William started towards Samuel. The vampire put his hand out, putting up an invisible barrier that stopped William in his tracks.

"I said I would sever your bond. That is what I did."

"Dead?" Jesse bent down and looked at the lack of shadow around him.

"You son-of-a-bitch, you didn't get rid of him!" William wound up and swung for Samuel's head. Far too slow for his target, he went off-balance and fell on his face.

Samuel shook his head at the man and stepped towards Jesse. "You are free, my son. It's time to move on."

"What do you mean, free? What the hell is goin' on?" Jesse wiped his sleeve across his nose to clean the snot that would have been there were he alive.

"We set you free. You are no longer tethered to this sad man." Samuel gestured towards William, who had gotten to his feet and was dusting himself off.

"I don't get it. You said I'm dead."

"Because you are, but you are also not. Only us and those that have touched the darkness can see you. You are little more than a wisp of a dream to the rest of the world."

"That don't make no sense."

"No, it doesn't," William chimed in.

Jesse looked from one man to the other, chewed his nonexistent lip and smiled. "You two are crazy, you know that? And another thing, *I beat you*, old man. Ha! I'm faster than you!" He clapped his hands together triumphantly.

"Come on, boy, you forget what just happened already?" William nodded at the hole in the boy's chest.

Jesse looked down, patted the area around the bullet hole, then stuck his fingers into the wound that wasn't really there. "Oh, shit. Shit!"

"We don't have time for this." Samuel walked away. "Come along, William. We have a lot to do before we get on our way."

"We can't just leave him here."

"Why not? There is not really anyone there that we will be leaving."

"What, you just create this thing and leave it to wander? What's wrong with you?"

"I didn't create anything. If anything, *you* created this apparition. All I did was separate the two of you and give the boy back his consciousness."

"That's even worse! He's dead and can't even affect the world around him."

"That is not my concern, and honestly, there is nothing he can offer to our endeavor."

"You asshole!"

Samuel spun, wrapped William's throat in his grip and hoisted him off the ground. "You need to be very careful here, Sheriff."

"Put—me—down." William rasped, tears welling in his eyes.

"I will put you down if you acknowledge that you have no power here. The only thing keeping you alive is your knowledge of the terrain beyond the hills because I don't believe this simpleton," he gestured towards Roy, "can guide me to Ruby."

Samuel gave a squeeze to remind William that he could snap his head clean off with little effort, then dropped the gasping sheriff.

"Well, that sure was sump'in," Jesse said, eyes wide and fingers still tracing the hole in his chest. "You're strong, mister."

Samuel walked away to his horse to check the saddle and supplies before they departed.

"You need some help?" Jesse said to William and reached down, his transparent hands passing right through William's arm. "What the hell?"

William shivered. "I told you, kid. You're dead. I'm sorry."

He turned to Samuel. "You never answered my question, Samuel. We're supposed to just leave this poor boy to wander around and spook people?"

Samuel stopped his tests on the straps and buckles of his saddle and scowled at the apparition. "Very well, take him along if you are so worried about him. Now come along, gentlemen," he nodded to Roy as well. "We have a long way to go before sunrise." He nudged his horse forward and Roy followed close behind.

William sighed and turned to Jesse. "I'm sorry, but this is complicated, Jesse. I have to go."

He went to his horse, grabbed the horn of his saddle and swung his weight into place on the tall horse's back. The animal chuffed and backed away from the barn.

"Good luck," William called back. "There's a whole world out there for you to explore and I have a feeling you have a thousand lifetimes to see it all." He gave a gentle squeeze to his horse. Then they were off.

A shadow among shadows, Jesse stood where he had died and watched the three riders shrink in the distance.

"A whole world," he said. He smiled and glided after the sheriff's party without effort. "Why not have a guide, then?"

Chapter 22 – Ruby's Snack

Ruby's meal was easy to overtake. She lifted the gape-mouthed old man off his feet and grinned at him. Her talons slashed through his ragged cotton shirt and paper-thin skin and tore into his guts. Still holding him up, the man screaming and flailing, she stepped into the room and kicked the door closed behind her.

With her free hand she wrenched onto one of his kicking legs. Then she punched through his guts, closed her hand around his spinal column and pulled upward, tearing the man in half.

Another maniacal grin, then Ruby brought her boot down on his skull and turned it into mush.

She shivered with the tingling rush of the kill. It had been a long day's ride and she had chosen to stop for the night at a small mining town. The hermit's cabin was not elegant, but it was quiet. There was only the man's emaciated dog and she had killed it quickly and noiselessly before she got to his door.

"Not the poshest, but it'll do," she said. She stretched her arms above her head and traced her bloodied fingertips across the bare beams of the low ceiling.

Time to dine. A bit gamey no doubt, but sustenance nonetheless. She leaned over the dead man's torso and started feeding.

Chapter 23 — The Road to Ruby

They rode in silence for the first hours of their trek through the crisp night. William donned his wool-lined leather jacket as the day's heat drifted off into the dusk, chased away by the rising moon.

There weren't many trails leading away from town that day, so they gambled on this being the right one. They rode west towards the next mining town, figuring Ruby would need to resupply and rest after her first day's travels. William suspected that Samuel could sense which direction Ruby had gone. The man had gifts William had never seen, not in all his time serving as a sheriff or traveling as a young cowhand and gunslinger.

The night was not too cold and the clouds stayed at bay. The bright moon lit their course. They moved slowly but deliberately through the night.

William thought of many matters as they rode along. He thought about what he was going to do when this was all over. He thought about meeting with Finn. Finn had stood up to Samuel and two others like him. He took down three of them and barely broke a sweat. What if they *could* bring him back? Could he convince Finn to turn on his one-time master again?

They rode through the night and into the early afternoon, William contemplating one scenario after another.

"I need to stop and rest for a while," Samuel said, finally.

"I thought we were trying to catch up to Ruby."

"We will catch her, just not today. And you want me as strong as I can be when we meet her."

"Fair enough. But where do you propose we pull off? There are no barns out this way, just hills and dirt."

"If you look close," Samuel pointed at a shadow in the surrounding hills, "you will see a cave in that rock face ahead." His hand dropped wearily as he slumped forward in his saddle.

"You know best, I guess. Hee-ya!" William spurred his horse on toward the hills, hoping to get the tired vampire to speed up after him. Time was wasting.

Chapter 24 — Ruby's Clean-Up

Ruby washed the blood off her naked body with a bucket of water she had pulled up from the well outside.

The tepid water washed over her soft skin, raising goosebumps with the chill that ran through the dim light of the spartan farmhouse. After her cleansing, she walked around the room to air-dry before heading to the saloon in town. She was not sure if she would stay long, but wanted to pay a visit to the sleepy village to gauge if it was worth a long stay.

Satisfied she was dry enough, she went to the corpse in the corner and admired her work. The old man had spilled his insides so easily, she could not decide if it was due to her infusion of strength from Finn or the frail frame of the man. He had tasted all right for such little work. She didn't mind the taste of humans, but did find it less than filling. They were like insects, while Finn and his brethren were the hearty stock she had grown to depend on over the centuries.

Reminiscing over her collective kills brought on a fresh wave of hunger. Ruby hurried over to the table where she had set her leather pouch with morsels left over from Finn and the others she had slain over the years. She untied the cord that sealed the pouch. She wet her fingertip and dipped it in the powder it contained along with the teeth, then inhaled the particles through her nostrils.

Her eyes rolled back, and she fell to the ground in a convulsive orgasm.

Chapter 25 — Jesse and the Other Side

The navy sky lightened as the sun chased the moon away with the approaching dawn. Jesse had grown accustomed to moving along with the hunting party. He didn't know how or why, but he found he could keep pace and eventually raise himself to a height where he could hold a conversation at eye level with the riders.

During the quiet moments when he was not trading barbs with Roy, he observed his various states of being. He was least transparent in the deep hours of the night. But as day came on, he became less and less solid-looking. Yet if he concentrated, he could bring himself back to near-solid again. By the time they reached the base of the hill below the cave, he had discovered that shifting from there and gone again was getting easier, but he wondered what would happen if he allowed himself to shift even further away from the world. Would he disappear for good? Would there be something in the beyond for him to go to?

He was not ready to explore that yet.

Chapter 26 – Rest in the Cave

The cave was cool and deep enough to shade Samuel throughout the heat of the day. The vampire slept while William reluctantly chatted with Roy and, on occasion, with the ghost who had tormented him for so long, now sociable enough.

Their voices echoed off the stone walls while their fire popped and crackled.

"Listen, you transparent ass," Roy told Jesse, "if you haven't even been with a woman, how can you sit there and argue about how these things work? Just because you fiddled your own shovel handle don't mean you know what it's for!"

"There is no way any girl would willingly kiss your pisser," the kid shot back. "No way!"

"Are you two gonna do this all day, 'cause I am gonna need some rest and this is not the bedtime story I want coloring my dreams." William shook his head.

"Why don't you back me up then," Roy said through his rotten-toothed smile. "Tell this smart-ass that if you pay the girls down at the tavern they would definitely kiss up on his tally-whacker and finish with a smile."

"Don't bring me into this. I just want to rest so we can get back on the road as soon as Samuel wakes up." William gestured at the dark mound curled up in the farthest corner of the cool cave. Samuel lay motionless as a boulder underneath his dark duster.

"I thought so. See, the sheriff won't even back you up with your dirty brain."

"You're just mad cause you can't get the thought of your ma slopping her face all over your pa's crotch is all."

The apparition stood and pointed a shaky transparent finger at Roy. "You shut your stinkin' mouth about my mama."

"In fact, I'm pretty sure I went to school with her. I remember exchanging some special moments with her out behind the schoolhouse."

"That's enough Roy," William said. "Leave the boy alone."

"I'm gonna kill you, you son-of-a-bitch!" Jesse launched through the air and descended upon Roy. But he merely passed through him and drifted to a halt on the other side of the smelly man. Roy cackled himself into a rasping wheeze.

William stood, took two steps forward and kicked Roy in the sternum. Roy stumbled back a good three feet and crashed down butt-first on the sharp gravel floor. He swore and swatted at the plume of dust around him as he clambered to his feet. He coughed and spat profanities at

William until he found himself staring down the barrel of the lawman's pistol.

"The kid may not be able to hurt you, but I sure as hell can."

Roy huffed in frustration. A thin stream of saliva dripped onto his boot toe. His hand shook above the handle of his own pistol. But he had lived long enough in Thrall to know the sheriff's reputation.

"You know I'm still good in a fight, Roy."

Finally, Roy cracked a crooked smile. "I was just bustin' his chops. Don't gotta take it so personal."

"I don't think you're exactly qualified to educate anyone on the ways of the world, let alone the wiles of women." William relaxed the hammer of his pistol. "Now, why don't you go out and find us something to eat while I get some rest?"

Roy spat. "I ain't afraid of you." Still, he turned and marched out of the cave.

"Why did you do that?" Jesse said, floating toward William. He stopped and hovered above the fire.

"He's an ass, kid. I don't tolerate people speaking out of turn with no intent of doing anything but stirrin' up trouble."

Jesse stared down at William with a quizzical look. "I don't git you, Sheriff."

William smoothed out his bed roll. "You don't have to. There's nothin' much to git, anyway." He lay down and closed his eyes.

While Jesse studied him from his place in mid-air, William drifted off to sleep.

Chapter 27 – Roy Pleads His Case

He woke to the smell of charred varmint and Roy talking to Samuel, the vampire listening as he drank from a tin cup. Even from a distance, William caught the iron scent of blood in Samuel's cup.

"Then the horse's ass kicked me and threatened to shoot me," Roy said.

Samuel nodded as he sipped on his rabbit's blood.

"So...what are you gonna do about it?"

"It's not my job to fight your battles for you," Samuel said, after a long pause. "In fact, if this happens again, I will possibly make a meal out of you for bothering me with your squabbles."

Roy watched dumbfounded as the tall figure walked away to join William at the fire.

Chapter 28 – Ruby Heads to Town

Thick smoke plumed from the doorway of the old man's burning shack. Ruby stepped out into the dusk, her pouch full of teeth tucked into Finn's saddle bags which she had slung over her shoulder. She called to her horse grazing in the pasture. The beast lifted its head and trotted over to her.

Cooing and stroking it, she secured the saddle bags in place. Then she made one last inspection of the horse and swung herself up into the saddle. A light kick to its side and they were off.

She rode toward the twinkling lights of the mining town ahead. Before she reached the bottom of the hill, she had already forgotten about the shack burning away in the night.

Chapter 29 – The Hunting Party Finds the Shack

"What do you think?" Samuel asked.

William studied the soot he'd sifted through his fingers.

"I think it doesn't make sense that this place burned down," he said. "The wood is dry, but the fireplace looks well cared for. So even if the owner left it unattended while he cooked, it shouldn't have sparked like it did."

He looked around at the charred remnants of human being strewn throughout the smoldering shack. "And the poor sap seems to be in pieces rather than burned alive. I have a feeling he met Ruby." He nodded at the kerosene lamp nearby.

"Not bad," Samuel said.

"What a bunch of horse shit," Roy said, and kicked at a tuft of grass.

"Horse shit or not, I think we're on the right track," William said. "She probably headed to that town up ahead."

"Then we should get moving," Samuel said.

William nodded. He turned to retrieve his horse.

Samuel took up stride next to him. "What do you propose we do if we find her?"

"Well now, ain't that up to you?"

"I know what we eventually need to do, but this creature is stronger than you can imagine. Having a bit of a plan at this point would be prudent. It would be best if I were at full strength and even better if we could employ the skills of my lost Finn, whose remains should still be in Ruby's possession."

"So, if she has them, where would she keep these remains?" William asked.

"Very close. Nothing will be more valuable to her. I believe she absconded with Finn's full rig, minus his knife which you've taken," he winked at the sheathed wooden blade hanging from William's hip, "so we should look for his horse and his saddle bags."

"Well then, let's get moving. We should be able to check the livery and any hitching posts that are occupied to see if she's there."

"Agreed."

The town was a hard hour's ride from the old man's ruined cabin. While Samuel and William discussed plans along the way, Roy and Jesse talked as they had not done on other occasions.

"So what do you think you're gonna git up to after all this is done?" The older man said.

"What do ya mean?" Jesse floated over next to Roy, gently bouncing up and down, mimicking the motion of a horse underneath. He had learned to manipulate his surroundings enough to be able to levitate higher and lower and even to adjust his speed to keep up with the horses.

"I mean, what do you think you'll do after this mess is finished up?" Roy spat a line of thick brown drool, coating his chin with it. He whipped it away with the back of his hand.

"I guess I'll stay on with y'all. Got nowhere else to be."

"Ha! You think there's gonna be an 'all of us' when this is done? Don't be such a child."

"I ain't no child!"

Roy's horse chuffed.

"Hey, settle down. You're scarin' my horse."

Jesse took note of the effect he had had on the animal. He might not be able to physically act upon his environment, but that didn't mean he couldn't mess with the world around him. "Sorry. Just don't like being talked down to, is all."

"It's fine, just be careful. I'm just trying to say that if our thing, whatever this is, goes to shit, you would be the one still hangin' around. It's not like she can rip your heart out, is it?" He stroked the horse's neck as it settled back into stride. "So, what'll you do?"

"Well, I'm not real sure. I mean, all I ever wanted was to be the fastest gun around. You know, make my ma and pa proud. Maybe learn to drink some whiskey and roll around with a girl. I never thought beyond that. I didn't have a chance to."

"Oh, Lordy. I'm the village idiot and even I know there's more out there than what you just described. There are bodies of water wider than the eye can see. There are things that would amaze you. Even bein' like you are."

Jesse frowned, staring ahead into the distance. He grew more transparent by the moment.

"Shit, kid, are you okay?"

"What? I'm fine." The apparition grew opaque again.

The two continued the final miles of their journey in silence as Jesse pondered the older man's words and the question of his purpose in the world.

Chapter 30 — Ruby's Night Out

Ruby stepped through the rickety saloon door into a dimly lit room with three round tables hewn from rough timbers and a raggedly constructed bar about seven feet long. The only patrons were a pair of drinkers at one table and a single rough rider attempting to coax the one female present to his place for the night. She wore a worn dress and chewed-up feather in her hair.

Ruby went to the bar. The woman at the other end of it scowled at her.

"You have whiskey back there, Slim?" Ruby asked the bartender.

"Got a couple bottles of watered-down Old Crow if you have the coin for it."

"The Old Crow will do."

Ruby slapped a couple of dollar coins on the counter. The bartender slipped them into his apron and pulled up a bottle of rotgut from behind the bar. "You want me to leave the bottle?" He set a glass next to the Old Crow.

Ruby nodded and poured herself a stiff drink. She downed it in a single swallow. She started to refill the glass when the tatter-dressed woman came over to her.

The woman took the glass and drained it. Then she slammed it back down between Ruby's hands.

"I'm sorry," Ruby said. "Would you like to join me for a drink, dear?"

"No need to be sorry. I have no problem tending to my needs as well as those of my boys here. You plan on being in town long?"

"Not long at all."

"Just so you know, I don't appreciate you coming into my bar without permission."

"Your bar. So you are the purveyor of this fine establishment?"

"I'm not, but I own the business that occurs on the other side of the drinks."

"Well, you have no problems from me. I'm just passing through and wanted to quench my thirst."

"It looks like you've quenched all the thirst you're going to tonight, so why don't you git on your way?" The woman grabbed Ruby's bottle and filled the glass almost to the top. She took the glass to drain it again when Ruby grabbed hold of her hand.

"Once was excusable. Twice is downright rude."

Ruby squeezed and the glass burst into shards that sliced into the woman's hand. Blood and whiskey splashed onto the bar top. The woman screamed. Ruby slashed the woman's neck with her own glass-laced hand.

The bartender gaped. "What are you doing?!"

Ruby grabbed the back of the man's head and slammed it down on the counter. His limp body dropped to the floor behind the bar.

The cowhand charged Ruby. She whipped her hand away from the dying woman's open wounds and splashed blood across his face. The spray blinded him. She lifted up her skirts and kicked the woman into him. The two of them tumbled across the floor and slammed into the opposite wall.

The two other men stared wide-eyed at the violence. After a moment, one of them raised his glass and Ruby raised her bottle in response.

The injured cowhand crawled out from under the weight of the dead woman.

Ruby went to him and smashed the bottle across his head. He swayed, losing consciousness. She looked into his blinking eyes and slammed the jagged mouth of the broken bottle into his temple. She watched the dead man crumple to the floor on top of the woman. Then she turned and walked around behind the bar.

She found a fresh bottle, plucked up three glasses and walked over to the remaining cowboys. She set down the bottle and glasses and sat across from them. She plucked the cork from the bottle and poured three glasses. She pushed two of the drinks across the table towards them.

"So. What else is there to do in this town for fun?" Ruby winked at the slack-jawed men, slammed her drink and poured herself another.

Chapter 31 – A Stroke of Good Luck

To call the place a town was being generous. The small assortment of ramshackle buildings had served as a waypoint for a nearby mine and the few farms that had cropped up over the years. The mine had dried up and so had the money. All that remained were a couple of businesses that catered to the farms and cowhands who had stayed on because they had no other prospects.

When William and Samuel arrived, they would have sworn the town was abandoned until they saw the soft lantern light that illuminated the saloon next to the post office and mercantile. The post office and mercantile were shut up tight for the night, but the watering hole was lit up and active. The three men and their ghostly companion hushed their animals and dismounted.

They saw Finn's tan horse tied up outside the saloon. The ornate saddle and saddle bags all but gleamed in the moonlight as they crept toward the horse. An unexpected sign in their favor. Ruby was close by.

As they got closer, the bar erupted in some sort of ruckus.

"Roy," William whispered. "go get a closer look at the bar and let us know if she's in there."

"No way. She'll take my head off!"

"You don't and I surely will," Samuel said.

Roy frowned, but moved towards the bar and stayed low as he peered through a side window. He nodded to them that she was in there. He kept watch while Samuel and William searched through the saddlebags on the uneasy beast that stood in wait for its new master.

They untethered the horse and hurried away from the commotion. The two men signaled for Roy to follow. He waved them off, fascinated by the violent scene on the other side of the greasy window. They signaled to him again, then went to their horses. With a huff, he bent low and scurried off to rejoin them.

Roy recounted the entire scene to them as the four rode far and fast into the night. Speed was everything now. Ruby would give chase when she discovered what had happened, and they had much to do before she caught up to them.

Chapter 32 — Ruby's Temper

Ruby stood on the wooden landing outside the saloon, a cowboy on each arm. She stared at the empty hitching post where her horse should have been.

"Somethin' wrong, darlin'?" One of the cowboys said.

Ruby blinked, stared at the men in turn, then back to the empty space where her horse should have been.

"What's the problem, honey?" The other cowboy said.

Ruby glared at the two confused men.

"My horse has been taken, boys."

"Don't fret darlin'. We'll get you a new horse in the morning."

She unsheathed her talons and snarled. "No, it means we will be cutting our evening short afterall, boys." Ruby's hands flashed across the two men's throats. They dropped to their knees, their lives spilling out between their fingers that wrestled to hold back the blood that spilled out in front of them. "But I appreciate you providing me with a quick meal before I go."

Chapter 33 — Back to the Cave

The men rode hard.

Once they cleared the buildings and were around the first hill, they opened up and pushed their horses with the urgency of survival on their breaths. They made good time and the sky was still dark when they spotted the mouth of their cave in the distance.

"We better have grabbed the right thing," William said, "'cause from the sound of it, we're not going to get a second chance at surprising her."

Samuel chuckled. "We have the right thing. Don't worry so much."

The horses grunted and foamed.

"What do we do next? Are you gonna create another ghost to spook her off or something?"

"Not exactly."

"I'm getting damn tired of your riddles, Samuel."

They rode their horses until they reached the cave.

They nearly collapsed as the men dismounted outside.

"Water the horses before they fall down dead," Samuel told Roy.

"Wha-what happened?" Roy slurred at them as he clumsily slid from his saddle. The smell of whiskey wafted from him as he swayed next to his horse.

"Jesus, Roy. Did you drink all my hooch?" William lifted the flap of the saddle bag and pulled out one of the many empty bottles. He looked into Roy's bleary eyes and dropped the bottle at his feet. He kicked it across the gravel floor.

"Yes...I mean...no?" Roy swayed in the moonlight. He let the empty bottle in his hand drop to his feet.

"It's of no concern now," Samuel said. "Roy, fetch water for the horses as well as a full kettle to boil on the fire."

The drunk man blinked at the request, working to reconcile the blurred figures that implored him to action. William walked up to him, grabbed his shirt collar and slapped him.

"Snap out of it. We need you to go to work. So, either get going or I'll keep slapping you till your cheeks bleed."

William shoved the drunk man backwards. Roy tripped on a log and landed hard on his rump. A cloud of dust erupted around him as he tried to get back on his feet.

"Enough, William," Samuel said. "As you say, we have work to do. Roy, do what William asked. It's the least you can do since you drank the rest of his night's sleep. And Jesse..." The ghost appeared next to Roy. "Go with him to make sure he doesn't drown himself in the creek. William and I have to prepare the rest of what we need for the ceremony."

Jesse gave Roy a mischievous grin. "Come on, Slappy. Time to go to work."

While the two left the cave, Samuel beckoned to William with his long finger.

"So you're tired of my riddles," the vampire said, as William stepped toward him. "In other words, you want answers. Here it is. We are going to attempt to bring back my old friend from the dead in hopes that we can take Ruby down with his help."

"You might have told me that sooner. But all right...though I get the feeling there's something you're still not telling me. Spill it."

Samuel reached into his pocket and pulled out a pouch. He tossed it to William. "Go ahead, open it."

William scowled at him, loosened the drawstring and looked inside the pouch. He shook it, then poured the contents into his hand. "Teeth. Jesus Christ, teeth! And what's this powder?"

"Be careful with those," Samuel said, as William put his fingers on one of the teeth. "We don't want to wake the wrong one."

Chapter 34 — Ruby Gives Chase

Ruby stood in front of the run-down bar where her exsanguinated playthings lay riddled with blow flies.

Thrall flashed in her mind every time she asked herself who had stolen her goods. Somehow this led back to that town. Did it have to do with Finn? Just the thought of her night with him warmed her and she licked at her lips instinctually searching for his long-gone taste on her skin.

Something to do with Finn. It had to be.

Yes, he had disposed of three others of his kind that night. She had enjoyed watching him work. It was such a pity to see the loss of the other vampires, though. Their teeth, along with his, would have sustained her for quite some time. Then a thought crossed her mind. What had happened to the other bodies? She'd been too distracted by Finn to have paid any real attention to their disposal. Those others had a connection to him. They had searched him out. Hunted him. No, not them. Him. *He* had led his minions to Finn. The tall, dark one. She remembered how calculated he had been, catching up to Finn in the bar. He was their leader.

That was who was after her. Somehow he had been revived in the night and had set out to hunt her, to retrieve Finn's remains. He needed Finn. Not the same way that she did, but she knew he would conquer death to have Finn back. She didn't blame him. She had tasted Finn's soul and felt him writhe inside of her. She knew the draw he had and even though she wanted him for her own sustenance, she could understand now why the older vampire had clawed his way back to the world and hunted her down.

She walked around the building and looked for tracks. There couldn't be too many fresh paths leading from the saloon. She would find her thieves' path and retrieve her missing essence, adding to her collection while she was at it. A vampire as resourceful as the elder would sustain her for decades.

She sharpened her senses with the intent of the hunt and began to tick off the least likely tracks until she was standing in the footprints of William, Samuel, and Roy. She set off with the gentle hint of dawn warming the cool early morning sky.

Chapter 35 — What's in the Pouch?

"What do you mean, 'the wrong one?'" William asked Samuel.

"Well, if we choose the wrong tooth, or teeth, we could bleed on the wrong one."

"What do you mean 'bleed?' Roy said. "Like when you came back?"

"Sort of, Roy, but it is more complicated with Finn."

"Why?"

"Because he has been gone longer, and let's be honest. There isn't much raw material to work with." Samuel gestured at the teeth in William's hand.

"So how do we know which teeth are his?" William asked.

"I'll need to give them a taste."

"Jesus."

Samuel waited a moment, then cackled. "I'm joking. Give me the teeth. I have a bond with Finn. I'll be able to feel which teeth are his."

"What kind of bond?" William said, and handed the teeth to Samuel.

"I made him what he was. Part of me is a part of him. I will able to sense him in the teeth."

"Then what? And be specific. Not like when you summoned the ghost kid."

"Hey!" Jesse said, appearing next to William.

"No offense," William said. "Well, Samuel? Then what?"

The vampire moved over to the circle of logs that surrounded the dead fire and sat.

"I will find Finn and do a simple resurrection ceremony similar to the process that brought me back to life the other night. "

"And then what?" William asked.

"I already told you, hopefully he can help us to take down Ruby. Assuming we can bring him back from the dead before she finds us. Now someone build a fire. I need to concentrate."

William shook his head and walked out of the cave. Roy went to work on the fire.

After the drunk lackey had gotten the flames going, Samuel opened the pouch and poured the contents into his hand. The ivory fangs twinkled in the firelight. He poked and prodded and sifted through them with his index finger. He flicked one and then another into the flames, discarding them as he searched for Finn's essence. Finally, he touched one that made him shiver. He put it in Roy's hand.

He threw two more teeth into the flames. Now only one was left. Two, counting the one he had given Roy.

"I'll take that back, if you please," he said.

Roy gave the tooth back. "So now what?"

"Now?" Samuel smiled. "You get to meet Finn."

Samuel plunged the two fangs into Roy's throat, then stemmed the spray of blood with his thumbs, pressing the fangs deep into Roy's neck.

William sat outside. The wind swirled, chasing a soft dust cloud through the valley below the lip of the cave. He envied that cloud of nothingness. No real purpose. Definitely no thought of whether it was going the right way or doing the right thing.

"You okay, Sheriff?" Jesse appeared next to him, more transparent in the daytime with the light shining through him.

William shivered. "Jesus, kid! Do you have to sneak up on me like that?"

"I don't have much choice."

"I know...just maybe announce yourself more subtle like, before you appear and start jabbering is all."

"Got it." Jesse mimicked a seated position next to him. "So do you?"

"Do I what?"

"Do you want company? I'm not exactly welcome inside and I'm not a big fan of Roy, anyway. Even being dead, I can smell his lack of a bath."

William chuckled.

"So what do I do anymore?"

"You got me, kid. I have no idea what I'm supposed to

do with all this, let alone what's next for you."

The dust devil below found a coyote to harass and gave chase to the skittish animal.

"I know you didn't mean for any of this, but I'm still pissed about what you did," Jesse said.

"Yeah. Me too, for what it's worth. I been kickin' my own ass all these years even with you haunting and tormenting me."

"How long has it been since you shot me? I kinda figured it wasn't too long, but the way you talk, we been at our little jig for a while."

"Boy, you brought me back to that barn every night, rain or shine, winter, fall, summer or spring for the past fifteen years or so. I stopped keeping track when the liquor started blurring the days together...but that seems about right."

Jesse looked at William as he watched the coyote below. "So I'm in my late twenties, then? Man, that messes with a person's brain."

"It messed with mine, for sure." William pulled a mostly empty bottle of whiskey from inside his vest, plucked the cork free and drained the contents in a single gulp. He winced at the sting of the harsh liquid and hissed in a breath. He relaxed and breathed out slowly, welcoming the sickly-sweet brew in his stomach.

Jesse scratched at his nonexistent chin a moment, then cleared his throat.

"Sheriff?"

"Yeah, Jesse."

"I think you need to know there's something going on in the cave."

William straightened. "What do you mean?"

"Samuel was not quite forthright about his plans."

"Oh. Well, shit, that's nothing new. I'd pluck out that vampire's weird-looking silver eyes if I could, he makes me so mad sometimes. What's he not being forthright about this time?"

"I hope you told Roy goodbye."

William snuck up on Samuel and cracked him on the back of the neck with a dry log. The wood split on impact and sent the vampire tumbling to the ground, dropping Roy in the process.

"That was uncalled for," Samuel said. He touched the wound, pulled his bloody hand back and licked it for whatever sustenance the blood could provide.

"Go to hell."

"I've been there and I'm trying to keep you from going there yourself." Samuel stood and licked his hand clean, then brushed the dirt from his clothes.

William knelt next to Roy. All that was left of him were faint, irregular twitches. William didn't particularly like Roy, but this was too much for him. "You son-of-a-bitch," he said.

The shot with the log had not satisfied him. Full knowing the vampire's greater strength, he charged Samuel, lifted him off his feet and drove him into the far wall. He pounded away at Samuel's sides, harder and faster until he spent himself. He stumbled back a couple feet, his fists held in front of him, shaking with anger.

"Are you quite done, Sheriff?" Samuel said. "Because I can do this all day, or I can tell you what all of this was about so we can move on to more important matters."

Roy's body jerked.

William watched as the flesh melted away from Roy's face, arms, and legs. His already booze-distended belly expanded. The shirt stretched beyond what the buttons could hold and popped off. The sound of cartilage and bone creaking under pressure resonated off the stone walls, followed by the pop of bones splintering, pressed outward by what was growing inside his torso. A single fingernail pierced the elastic skin from inside, followed by a hand and then the whole arm. The bloody arm struggled to free the rest of itself from its Roy-shaped casing. A second arm ripped free and joined the first. Soon a creature stood coated in the afterbirth of Roy's last meal and pieces of chewed-on organs.

A howl of agony, anger, and satisfaction echoed through the cave. Finn stood before the two men, naked and glistening. He raised his screams to the moon that wasn't up yet, then collapsed to the floor, panting and unconscious, exhausted from his resurrection.

"Jesus Christ," William said.

"If you say so," Samuel said. "But you see, Sheriff, everything I do has a purpose, no matter how bad it looks. Even Roy's pathetic life was the catalyst for something great."

Chapter 36 – A Look Back at the Finn That Was

Finn's life consisted of daily chores and caring for his sick mother. The father he had never known rarely entered his thoughts, aside from the romanticized daydreams that crept into his evenings by the fire, as he listened to the cracks and pops from the hearth.

Many evenings he would read to his mother, his warm voice accompanied by her rasping breaths and coughs. He couldn't count the times he had read through the small number of books they had acquired over the years. *Little Women*, *Oliver Twist*, *Moby Dick*, and when she slept, the stories of Edgar Allan Poe.

His quiet days ended the night she coughed to death in his arms. Another victim of consumption.

After his mother's death, Finn kept his daily routine,

but his loneliness ate away at him. His trips into the township grew more frequent. They became less about the necessity of goods and services and more about the need for company. He got to know the mercantile owner, the postal worker and the townsfolk. His desire for company outweighed his need to tend his plot of land. Soon his crops dwindled with little more than enough yield to keep him from starving through the winter, though not enough to sell the excess so as to purchase the next year's seed and provisions.

He and his mother had lived simply, and her frugality had left him with enough money that he could quench his loneliness at the saloon. He drank his way through the next year with little to show for his poor judgment.

Each morning he would stumble home, the previous night's drunk still hanging over him, do the barest of work, splash water on himself to lessen the ever-present stink, then walk back to the saloon. His self-loathing grew with every morning he woke up to the harsh daylight, sprawled in the dirt outside the saloon.

One night, the fog of whiskey was settling over his vision when the saloon hushed. A stranger sauntered into the room, tall, clean-cut and dressed in a flowing black duster.

The man went to the bar and stood beside Finn.

"Evening, stranger." The bartender set a glass in front of the new customer.

"Evening, sir."

"What can I getcha?"

"Would it be too much to ask for a beer?"

"Not too much to ask, but we aren't exactly outfitted for such fare."

"What do you have on hand?"

"Whiskey, unless you're a bit soft, and then I have a couple bottles of wine collecting dust for the lady-folk." The scruffy man grinned.

"Whiskey is fine."

The stranger grabbed the bottle from the bartender, yanked the cork free and sloshed its contents into his glass. He slid a shiny quarter across the bar top.

Finn watched him slug down a healthy gulp of the vile, powerful stuff.

"Anything I can help you with, kid?" the tall man said without looking at Finn.

"Oh, um, help me with?"

"The way you've been eyeballing me since I came in, I'd swear there was something you wanted to ask of me."

"N-no. It's just...we don't get your kind that often around here."

The man fixed his silver eyes on Finn. "My kind?"

"Sorry. I mean...someone so refined, is all."

The stranger chuckled. "Refined, am I?" He drained his glass, tapped the counter with it and set out a dime. While the bartender refilled his glass, he extended a long, pale hand at Finn. "My name is Samuel."

Finn gawked, then squeezed Samuel's hand. "Finn. Whoa! That's quite the grip, mister."

"You too, son. Are you a farmer?"

"Used to be before my ma died. Now it's just hard to get myself going like I used to."

"Why is that?"

Finn took a healthy swig from his drink. "Well, it's like there's no one to do it for anymore, ya know? I used to do it to take care of her and she used to cook and clean up after me. Now it's just me and I don't know what to do." He took another drink and realized he hadn't spoken to anyone about this before. There was something about Samuel that put him at ease.

"I understand that. It's hard to push through the day's drudgery when no one can share in the spoils of your work."

Finn smiled, chuckling to himself.

"Mister, can I buy you a drink?"

"Indeed, son, you can."

The two men talked and laughed into the earliest hours of the morning. Finally, the bartender shuffled them out the door, relieved that Finn hadn't puked on his floor as he usually did.

They held each other up, singing and laughing and fumbling into the night.

The two came to the edge of town and faced each other. Finn burped back the urge to spew bile across the front of his new friend. "Wh-where you stayin' while you're in town?"

Samuel stretched out his arm to steady the young man. "Nowhere in particular. I usually just find the nearest boarding house, but this little town doesn't seem to have such an enterprise. I figured I would venture to the west a bit and find a tree to rest my head under tonight. The weather seems reasonable and I need to be on my way early anyway and no better way to get on the

road then with the morning sunlight kissing me hello."
He beamed at Finn, his pristine teeth winking with the
soft glow of moonlight.

"That's ridiculous," Finn said. "Come to my place.
You can at least have a roof over your head and a warm
breakfast before heading on your way."

"I wouldn't want to put you out."

"Nonsense. It's a quick ride out past the edge of
town." Finn staggered towards the pair of horses secured
in front of the bar.

"Well then, lead the way, fine sir." Samuel curtsied.
The two laughed and were on their way.

The two men entered the home. Finn stoked the fire
back to life while Samuel unburdened himself. He laid his
saddle bags across a kitchen chair and draped his black
leather duster over top.

Finn stood and turned around. Samuel was nose to
nose with him.

"Whoa, hey there, friend," Finn blustered, taken
aback by Samuel's closeness.

Samuel placed his soft, cold lips on Finn's. He wet the
young man's mouth with his stale breath and flicked the
inside of his lip with his coarse tongue.

After a moment, Finn pushed away and stumbled
backwards, his head swimming from booze and lack of
oxygen.

He was not sure if he was embarrassed that he had
allowed the kiss to happen, or because a part of him
swelled with excitement. "Sorry, mister, no offense, but

around here we don't get so affectionate with our friends of the same trouser cut."

"There is no need to be shy, my boy. There is no one here but you and I." Samuel matched Finn's steps as the young man backed away from him.

Finn backed into his cook stove, the metal of the rusted cabinet groaning from the collision. "It's not that I'm shy. I-I-I mean, I am shy, but that's not it." He kept an arm's length between him and Samuel. "Maybe you should stay in the barn tonight."

Samuel closed the space between them, his weight pressed into Finn's outstretched hand. The two halted, barely half an arm's length between them. Adrenaline coursed through Finn's veins, sobering him. He stared into Samuel's silver eyes.

"You don't have to be scared, Finn."

"I'm not scared. I'm just, I don't know." He pushed Samuel back and walked away.

Samuel grabbed his elbow and pulled him close, his breath teasing Finn's ear. His rough cheek scraped the side of Finn's face as he pulled him close. "Given a chance, I can show you wonders that you have never dreamed possible."

"I'm not sure the wonders you offer are something I'm interested in exploring." Finn tried to wriggle out of his guest's tight grip.

"We'll see."

Samuel wrapped his arm around Finn, bared his fangs and bit into the young man's neck. Finn struggled against Samuel's iron hold. Samuel moaned with the exhilaration of tasting his prey. Finn wept and fought to scream but the sound never came. He struggled as long as he had strength, but that did not last long. There was but a trickle left when Samuel broke the bond and spun the limp body in his arms around to face him. Finn's eyes fluttered.

"Are you afraid?" Samuel asked.

"Y-y-yesssss...."

"Then let me show you the true strength that courses through me."

Samuel let loose with one hand, balancing Finn in one arm. He swiped his free hand across his fangs, opening a gash across his smooth skin. Black blood gathered in a thick stream and Samuel held the hand above Finn's mouth. The weak boy coughed at the salty tincture, helpless to fight the vampire's offering as it oozed down his dry throat, coating his insides with death and the stench of evil and the familiarity of his own blood being fed back to him.

It didn't take long for the transformation to take hold. Within seconds he went from retching to lapping at the splashes on his chin from Samuel's hand.

"That's enough, my boy," Samuel said, finally.

Finn ignored him and latched on, hunger taking hold.

"I said, That's enough!" Samuel flung his feral recruit loose. Finn sprang to all fours. He snarled through the dust and the blood ridden stream of saliva that drooled past his lips.

Samuel stood firm in the middle of the room. "Don't fret. We will find you a meal, but I am your master, not your lunch."

The feral instinct that had taken hold of Finn

subsided and he slowly stood. He backed away, looked at his bloody hands. "What...what have you done to me?"

"I put you on top of the food chain. You're welcome."

Samuel winked and walked out the door to sleep away the coming day in Finn's barn.

Finn snarled, watching him go, then sniffed at the air and ran his tongue over his teeth. Long, sharp. Not human teeth.

Not human anymore.

He screamed.

Chapter 37 - Finn's New World

Finn woke to the thud of boots next to his face. He jolted up. Pain ripped through him. He grabbed at his arm, his leg, his gut. Samuel stood over him, looking amused.

"Did you sleep well?"

"Go to hell."

"We should get you cleaned up."

"Why?" Finn winced at the pain as he stood.

"Because you're hungry and it's better to get something in your stomach early rather than let the pangs linger."

"Hungry? Right now, I'm just thirsty."

"Same thing."

Samuel flung fresh clothes at him. Finn grumbled. He marveled at the chaos surrounding him. He had wrecked his place with his bare hands. He should have been covered in bruises and cuts. But any pain he felt was inside, and that was more tolerable the more he moved around. "What time is it?"

"It's time to move on. We need a couple of horses since you scared all of yours with your caterwauling."

Finn followed Samuel out the front door.

The idea of feeding, as Samuel had fed on him, turned his stomach. Then he realized it was not the idea of killing that nauseated him, but the idea that for some reason he didn't mind the idea of killing. That shouldn't be right, but his brain had reconciled the idea. Killing and life would be synonymous. But was that always the way? He had killed before. He had trapped the cattle in the gallows and looked in their eyes as he passed his curved blade across their throat in order to feed him and his mother. Were the humans his new cattle? Or was there another way?

"You must have questions," Samuel said over his shoulder.

"Why me?"

"Real questions."

"Fine. Where are we going?"

"You need to feed. We're going hunting."

"I should've grabbed my rifle, then." Finn turned back to the shack.

Samuel grabbed his arm and spun him back around. "You won't need it."

"I don't understand."

"You will."

The two walked in silence. Finn struggled with his new, heightened sense impressions. The sounds of animals on the other side of a hill. The scratching of a snake's scales rubbing across the fur of its recent bunny kill. The smell of the sleeping flora of the desert. His stomach rumbled. His head pounded. The sharp images of every grain of sand, the ridges of pebbles like boulders, the hairs on the back of Samuel's hand raised like a forest of birchwood…

"You'll adjust," Samuel said. "Just breathe and try to slow down how much you take in."

"Jesus, it's like snorting broken glass."

"Indeed. You're being birthed into a new self. You can see more, hear more, feel more. The world you knew was a dull reflection of the one you're now part of."

Finn sighed. He closed his eyes for a moment, then opened them and breathed in four, out four, over again and again. The pattern took over and his nerves calmed to a hum.

It didn't take long before they caught the sounds of village night life up ahead.

"Where are we headed?"

"We need to get you a drink, Finn."

"I thought we were looking for a meal."

"Same thing."

"So the saloon then?"

"No. The saloon has too many people. We just need one."

Finn didn't like the sound of that, but his hunger was the one bodily sensation he couldn't calm down.

They wandered past the saloon, past the darkened windows of the mercantile and post office. The smell of horse flesh called to him, their heavy bodies coursing with the sustenance he craved. He felt his canines shift at the scent. He swallowed back the saliva on his tongue and measured the new teeth with his tongue.

Now Finn homed in on the scents of the town. From the earth under his boots to the woman crossing the street. His stomach stirred. He imagined attacking her and lapping at her until she was raw and stripped of skin. The only problem—aside from her being human and not something the vestige of old Finn would ever want to harm, let alone eat—was she was swollen with child, he could smell it, not just see it.

Then both men heard the scrape and thump of a box being dragged across the wooden planks of a schoolhouse porch.

From the shadows, they watched as a lone schoolmarm inched her heavy box of books towards the school entrance.

Samuel grabbed Finn's arm. "I can smell your hunger, boy. But we have to do this smart. You can't just take her down like a deer on an open field."

Finn pulled his arm free. "Fine. So how *do* monsters like us handle this situation?"

"Why don't we start by offering our help? You know...like gentlemen."

Finn watched the woman a few more moments and sighed. "Jesus. This is horrible, Samuel."

"The hunger is powerful. For a while yet it will be my job to keep you out of trouble."

Finn breathed and listened to his heart beat. It slowed as he gained control of his urges. He made his pupils shrink back to a more human appearance. "So what? We just walk over and offer to carry her crate in for her? What if we scare her?"

"Then we'll have to back off and go after her again

with a less subtle approach. We'll leave it up to her how she wants to be served up."

"Oh, God."

"It will all work out. Just pay attention and we'll get you fed."

Samuel chuckled and slapped Finn on the back. They walked toward the struggling woman.

"Excuse me, ma'am," Samuel said, "may we be of service to you this evening?"

The schoolmarm started at the two men standing before her.

"Beg your pardon, miss," Finn said.

"It's okay. Usually I'd pass on your offer, but I must say this shipment of books is quite the task for someone of my size to tackle."

"Allow us, then." Samuel bowed and went to one side of the crate while Finn went to the other.

Still new to his strength, Finn had to catch himself from flinging the box up in the air, it felt so light. "Where to, miss?"

"Right this way." The schoolmarm pointed them towards the dark recess of the schoolhouse. Samuel kicked the door shut behind them.

They took the crate to the front of the classroom.

"Right here is fine." The woman gestured next to the desk and they set the crate down with a scraping thud.

"Thank you again, gentlemen."

"It was our pleasure, ma'am," Samuel said, stepping around the desk and flanking the woman with Finn on the other side.

Finn turned away, breathing hard.

"Are you okay?" the schoolmarm asked him.

He turned around again. His black eyes bored into her. She screamed and backed away, but Samuel stood behind her and held her shoulders.

"What are you waiting for, boy?" He said.

Finn shook his head. "I...can't..."

"You have to. There is no going back."

"There has to be another way."

"Even if there were, she's seen us."

"No, I won't say a word," the woman said. "I have no idea what you're talking about. Just let me go!"

"She's lying, Finn. It *has* to be done."

"I can't!"

But as he fought his abominable urges, his feet moved him towards her. He drew closer, tears streaked down his face. This was not the scenario he had justified in his imagination. He had likened the hunt to the killing of livestock on the farm. He had tried to dehumanize his future victims by raising himself up in the food-chain. But battling the incessant hunger that gnawed at his insides was proving futile.

He stared into her horror-stricken eyes and lapped at the salty tears that seasoned her flesh.

Her soft whimpers of, "please" squeaked past her strained vocal cords. Smelled the peppermints she crunched on throughout the day on her breath that sweetened the fear that wafted from her.

For a moment his eyes returned to their human appearance. Then they went black again and he reared his head back, sprouting fangs.

"I'm sorry," he said, and tore into the woman's throat.

He fed hastily, sloppily, mangling the flesh so that he lost as much blood from the wound as he drank. At last, she grew weak and Samuel loosened his grip. He kicked Finn away and turned the limp girl around in his arms to lap up what little sustenance she could still offer.

Renewed strength coursing through him, Finn howled.

Samuel dropped the limp body and slapped him across the cheek. "Are you crazy? The town will hear. We have to be a little more discreet."

The two stood across from each other. Finn panted and hissed past a viscous layer of blood and saliva. The salty sweet taste of death wafted off his breath.

"What have you done to me?"

"I made you the best version of you."

"No! You made me a killer!"

"We are all killers my boy."

They took the books from the crate, arranging them throughout the room as they thought the schoolmarm might, then laid her body inside the box. Using the straw leavings from the books' packing, they mopped up the drippings from Finn's sloppy kill. The bloody remnants were dropped into the box on top of the dead woman and the lid was secured.

They buried the box outside of town. They returned to Finn's home for the last time, shutting out the first streaks of daylight.

Finn splashed water across his face. He fought the urge to lap at the watered-down traces of blood in the basin.

"We need to work on your efficiency when you kill," Samuel said from across the room.

Finn slumped over the basin. "I can't do this, Samuel."

"Of course, you can. I'm here to guide you to your better self." Samuel came up behind him and laid his hand on Finn's back.

Finn wanted to shrug it away and grab hold tight at the same time. He let Samuel trace his hand up his neck and into his thick black locks. He pressed his face into the crook of Samuel's shoulder. He sobbed.

"There, there," the vampire said. "It will all be all right. You need to rest. Let's lie down and we'll tackle the next steps tomorrow."

Samuel guided him to the bed and laid him down. The two rocked themselves to sleep in each other's arms.

"It's time to move, Finn. We need to find nourishment and get on the road before it gets too late."

"Do we have to eat every night? I still feel satisfied from the girl."

"Not every night, but since we have to travel, it's best to fill up. It might be a day or two before we run across another opportunity for a meal."

"Who are we going to hunt tonight?"

"To the west of town, there's a small cattle ranch. I believe a husband and wife live there. They'll have supplies and horses for us after we've eaten."

"So we're thieves now, as well."

They freshened up and Finn looked around his boyhood home for the last time.

He headed out the door behind Samuel. He ducked as a blazing torch flew past his head. It landed on Finn's soiled linens and lit the dry tinder of the shack on fire.

"What are you doing?"

"You can't come back here. I'm just facilitating a more permanent exit."

Samuel walked off in the direction of the cattle ranch. Finn stood, mouth open, eyes brimming with tears as his childhood homestead burned. The flames poked through the cracks in the roof and the blaze roared in his ears.

Chapter 38 — Terror at the Farmhouse

As close as the other ranch was, Finn had never met the owners. He had lived so near and never shared a greeting, let alone a meal. Now his neighbors *were* the meal.

Samuel had made sure to detail the various ways and tactics for subduing and draining victims while they made their way through the evening in route to their dinner. Finn was both squeamish and intrigued as Samuel outlined basic human anatomy and the inner workings of the heart along with other human delicacies, he would soon be introduced to along their journeys.

The night air was thick with the chatter of nervous livestock. Samuel beckoned Finn forward. "Stay close. Cattle don't tend to like our kind and we don't want them giving us away."

The two sped across the distance with barely a cloud of dust raised.

Thick white smoke puffed from the stone chimney

and the sounds of metal utensils scraped across plates inside signaling it was dinner time. Samuel and Finn nestled in on either side of the orange glow of the window and peered in unnoticed by the occupants.

The couple sat across from each other, finishing off their meal of stew and fresh baked bread. The smells permeated the wood walls, coating the night air with the thick scent of meat and carrots swimming in thick gravy.

Before, Finn would have coveted the salty tang of the home cooked meal. But now he thought only of biting into the soft neck of the woman, the zesty smack of warm blood and the slurp of sweet marrow as he hollowed out her bones.

"What happens if we eat regular food?" Finn asked, his hushed whisper imperceptible to the quiet couple on the other side of the wall.

"I don't recommend it. I once shared a bowl of stew with a man before I killed him. The next morning, I had awful pains and spewed it back up." Samuel looked at Finn mischievously, "but liquor and sex seem to be the indulgences left over from our past lives."

Samuel signaled to follow him but stopped him as the door to the house swung open. The man's shadow stretched across the porch and out into the prairie. He took a step out and the hiss of a match sizzled in the night air. He lit and puffed a glowing ember of tobacco to life in his seasoned cob pipe.

They huddled in the shadows watching the quiet man puff. Swirls of smoke plumed from his pipe, circling his head, carried off by the gentle breeze. The tall man tamped the final glowing remnants from his pipe and returned to the solace of his home.

Samuel gave Finn's arm a squeeze and the two stood. "I will distract them at the window. Wait for my sign before you bust in."

"What is the sign?"

"You will know."

Finn moved toward the porch. Samuel took position under the glow of the open window.

A scraping sound, out of place from their familiar nighttime noises, called the couples attention to the window. There was no tree next to the house to attribute the soft knocks and scratches. The cattle were restless but secured and there was no other wildlife brazen enough to venture so close to their home.

They wondered what could cause the repetitive etching. The broad-shouldered man shrugged and lifted himself up, his rocker groaned under his muscled weight, and he strode to the window to investigate the noise.

The woman tensed, "Jeb, what is it?"

"Probably just a coyote circling in for a look. I'm sure it's nothing." He neared the open window and stared into the black night.

He strained his eyes to see past the safety and glow of their warm house. The hairs on the back of his neck stretched upward. The scratching continued. The chaotic rhythm did not resemble digging or anything that he would associate with the activities of a creature investigating new surroundings. It started and stopped at random, as he stood looking out, the sound grew stronger.

"What do you see Jeb?"

"Nothing. It's black as coal out tonight."

"Why don't you just close the window and come back and read." Her voice quivered.

Jeb ignored her and investigated further. The scratching stopped. He strained his eyes searching the dense black night for its source. He took another step and reached for the shutters. The scratching bit at his ear and he gave a little jump and it stopped.

Jeb crept closer. He set his heavy hands on the sill of the window and leaned forward. He willed his eyes to adjust to the void beyond the window. The cattle brayed and shuffled in the pen nervously. He scanned right and left. He leaned out the window further, craning to locate the scratching.

"Jeb dear. Close the window and come back."

He held his breath so he could focus on the direction of the sound. But it halted and the cattle calmed.

Jeb let out a sigh and chuckled at his child-like fear. He stood and turned to his wife. He smiled at her and shrugged his shoulders, disarming her nerves with his relief.

Then he was gone, ripped from the room through the window as if swallowed by the dark.

The front door burst open; the metal bolt ripped from its housing as Finn kicked into the room.

The woman screamed as her husband's hand flopped over the windowsill dragging his bloodied face from the dark. His bloodshot eyes bulged in terror. "Ru-u-u-n." He gurgled. A wiry hand slapped down on his forehead and pressed his head to the side. Samuel's face emerged from the dark. His fangs were stained crimson from his initial sampling of Jeb. His black eyes glistened in the firelight as he clamped onto Jeb's neck. The man rasped in fear and agony as he was dragged away.

The woman's vocal cords rattled from strain as she screamed her last goodbye to her love.

Ravenous, Finn strode toward the howling woman. He plucked her up and tossed her to the floor. She futilely fought to fend him off as he positioned for the kill. He straddled her, pinning down her arms under his knees. He leaned toward her yells in search of the supple valley of her neck that Samuel had directed him to earlier. Her head whipped back and forth as she fought for freedom.

Finn grabbed her hair and pressed her down, exposing her elegant neck. He was determined to make the kill quick and efficient. His bite was not graceful, but it was true. Her screams and wriggling subsided more quickly than with the schoolmarm. With every pump of the heart, he drank her in. He lapped up the final droplets as her heart pushed the last ounces of life into his mouth.

There was little gnashing of the flesh this time while he siphoned her salty soul into his own body, one gush at a time. He was a fast learner.

Samuel stood over his protégé. "Much better my boy." He ruffled Finn's hair as if he were a schoolboy who had just learned his multiplication tables. Finn grinned in the afterglow of his successful feeding. His veins tingled from the infiltration of the young woman's blood mingling with his own.

The two left the small farmstead with full bellies, fresh horses, and saddle bags filled with whatever money and supplies they could scavenge. They road off into the night in search of shelter.

Chapter 39 — Finn Departs

Samuel and Finn made a good team. They managed to keep a low profile wherever they went.

Their wealth grew, and their affections, cultivated by their mutual hunger and Finn's inexperience, grew as well. But Finn's wariness of Samuel's intentions was always in the back of his thoughts. He didn't always agree with his mentor's choice of targets. The beginning of the end was when Samuel decided to invest in the Black Cross Ranch.

The large parcel of land was easy to buy with the funds stolen from their feedings. It was not the purchase that bothered Finn; it was Samuel's compulsion to grow their brood. He got worked up after especially violent feedings and waxed on about the possibility of growing their family. Finn was accustomed to the two of them sharing their adventures and feedings. The idea of expanding their reach with more followers, as Samuel referred to them, made him nervous.

One day, Samuel visited a dude ranch without Finn to get more recruits. He showed up at the Black Cross Ranch exhausted and with five new followers in tow.

Finn confronted him, but the new recruits restrained him. He had grown faster and stronger than Samuel over the years so that the elder vampire leaned increasingly on his recruits when his first one lost control.

As Samuel grew his tribe, so did Finn's willingness to end him. He planned and gathered his strength.

Finally, he felt it was time to act.

At dawn as the others settled in for sleep, Finn donned his duster and wide-brimmed hat. He went out into the dawn's light and went to work. He secured the doors and windows of the ranchhouse and the barn from the outside. He painted the walls of the compound's buildings with pitch. His duster and hat protected him from the daylight as he worked.

His final step was to strap a keg of gunpowder to his horse. He punched a hole in the keg and led his horse through the compound, trailing a maze of explosive powder. Then he mounted his horse and trotted away from the ranch, gunpowder still spilling behind him.

The trail ran out five-hundred yards from the ranch. Finn dismounted. The heat of the late afternoon sun bore down on him. He struck a match across the back of his saddle and dropped it onto the black trail that led back to the ranch. He watched the flame snake its way back to the compound.

Samuel had no one to blame but himself. He taught Finn to be ruthless and since Samuel and his minions were less than alive to Finn, he had no sympathy for them. The creatures' tortured screams rose along with the flames. Finn watched the ranch burn for a while, then mounted his horse and rode west as the sun sank below the hills.

He carved his own myth in the wild world that lay in front of him. He chose to kill only when he needed to, and he knew there were plenty of wicked men and women in the world to quench his thirst. When they weren't available, he learned the secret Samuel held back for so long. The blood of animals, though not as sweet, granted him just as much life and power. He could feed with a clean conscience and live among those he once called kin again.

Chapter 40 - Finn Reborn

Finn stood ankle deep in what was left of Roy.

"What the hell?" William choked back the bile in his throat.

"I believe you have met Finn." Samuel gestured to the naked man.

Finn examined the film of viscera and innards that clung to him.

"What did you do?" William asked Samuel.

"I just gave us a fighting chance. You're welcome."

Samuel stripped a horse blanket from one of the logs around the fire ring. He draped it over Finn's glistening shoulders.

Finn punched Samuel in the chest and sent the older vampire flying back into the stone wall. Samuel dropped to the floor and pulled himself up to all fours. The two snarled and chomped at the air.

William stepped between them. "Whoa, whoa!" He waved frantically at the creature they had resurrected. "Finn! Do you remember me?"

Finn stopped and considered tearing through William to get to Samuel.

He was a vision of horror. His eyes were onyx orbs full of hunger and pain and his hair was matted with the stuff of his rebirth.

"Yes," he said, after a long pause studying the man who stood between him and revenge. "You're the sheriff."

"Yes. That's right. You can call me William."

Finn snarled over his shoulder at Samuel.

William caught the gesture and raised his hand. "I know this is difficult, but I need you to focus on me. How about we get you cleaned up a bit?"

Finn sheathed his fangs and nodded. "Okay. But keep that thing away from me." He turned his back on the sheriff and Samuel, pulled the blanket off his shoulders and began to scrape the gore off his body.

Jesse watched the altercation for a moment, then caught movement from the pile of Roy by the fire. A specter rose, the world shining through its transparent form.

"Roy...is that you?"

The shimmering vision ignored the boy.

"Roy!"

A blinding light split open above the apparition. Jesse had never seen Roy look so clean and at peace. He watched in awe as Roy looked up at the bright chasm.

Jesse rushed forward, curious if the gateway was meant for them both. He wondered if he would be granted ascension like his foul-mouthed friend.

Roy drifted upwards. Jesse reached him and attempted to grab onto the transparent feet. Instead of being carried along with Roy into the bright void, he passed right through the ghost, just as he passed through the physical world he was trapped in.

Roy kept ascending, at the last second looking down at Jesse. With a mischievous grin, he extended his middle finger and winked. Then, as quickly as the tear in space had opened for him, it was gone.

Jesse was heartbroken. Was he not given the chance to move on, or had he somehow missed it?

Did he really want to move on?

He floated in the dark, pondering his existence while the others bickered in the background.

"I didn't need your help." Samuel dusted off his clothes while Finn wiped himself clean.

"Yes, you did. A thinking creature is no match for a rabid killer, no matter how smart you think you are."

"He's not as tough as he appears."

"I'm pretty sure he is, or you wouldn't have gone through so much to bring him back, especially after he already bested you once." William left Samuel.

Samuel rubbed at the sore spots where he had connected with the wall.

Meanwhile, Jesse chatted with Finn, asking what it

was like where he had gone.

"it was black." Finn scrubbed at a stubborn patch of goo on his elbow with the abrasive wool of the blanket, his pale skin reddened as he worked it clean.

"Is that all? Is that because you had no soul?"

"It's probably because I was killed by a demon who stole my essence."

"Huh." Jesse thought of the afterlife that he would never know. He wrestled with the idea that even after the world was gone, he would be a vaporous cloud floating around in the abyss, alone and timeless.

William gathered a set of fresh clothes from one of the saddle bags, joined the duo by the fire and dropped the bundle next to Finn. "Thought you might want some clothes. The cave gets a bit drafty."

Finn nodded appreciation and went to the task of scouring his hair with the blanket.

"I'm sorry for the rude awakening," William said, gesturing to the oozing body that littered the far side of the fire pit. "I didn't know that was Samuel's plan."

"I don't blame you, Sheriff. I know Samuel. His skills of holding back just enough until it's too late to stop whatever he has cooked up in his twisted brain are considerable." He pulled on the pants from the bundle.

"Do you know why we brought you back?"

"I can guess, although I'm not sure I understand how Samuel is walking and talking. I put him down myself back at the Braided Pony."

"That was partially due to Roy." William gestured to the gooey mess that birthed him. "But that's neither here nor there. I'm pretty sure we're in big trouble."

"I can guarantee that." Finn slipped the linen shirt over his head; a gentle stain of pink from his hair colored the cream-colored fabric. "The question is how long we have before trouble finds us. Even with Samuel and me together, Ruby is too powerful for me to take down in my state." He slumped down onto a log, brushed the blood-clotted dirt from his toes and wrestled a pair of leather boots onto his feet.

"What do you mean?" Jesse asked.

"You been born recently, boy? It's tiring to rip yourself out of another body."

William noted Finn's sunken eyes and slumped posture, watched his short, uneven breaths. "I would guess as much," he said, "to look at you, Finn, no offense. What can we do for you?"

Finn cocked his head and looked hungrily at William. "I'm pretty sure Samuel brought you along as a second course."

William tensed, but stared right back at Finn. "You're saying all along he wanted to birth you with Roy and strengthen you with me, is that it?"

"Looks like I might have company soon." Jesse chuckled.

Finn shrugged. "You have no need to worry, Sheriff. I have no plan to end your life any time soon."

"Then what do you propose?"

"The problem with Samuel is that he is too proud and sadistic to partake in a lower form of life than humans."

As if on cue, a rumbling echoed from the far recess of the cavern.

Chapter 41 – Ruby Tracks Her Prey

The morning poured down on Ruby with its unwelcome rays of light. She squinted under the wide brim of her hat. Though she was not as allergic to the sunlight as her vampire cousins, she didn't enjoy the harsh daylight that nipped at her through the heavy leather duster.

She had tracked her prey through the night. One man and two vampires. The man would make a reasonable snack, but she would take her time with the vampires. She'd torment and feed off them for days.

Visions of flaying, biting and decapitating her new playthings left her warm and tingly. She licked her lips with anticipation and quickened her stride in the direction of their scent. Given that one of the vampires smelled familiar, she figured the reason for the theft was to resurrect one of her past victims. With the activities at the Braided Pony so fresh, she supposed that Finn's foe from that evening was the one behind her troubles.

Ruby had heard that certain vampires had found ways to dodge death's scythe even when dispatched in the traditional ways.

She quickened her step even more, driven by curiosity and hunger. A soft plume of dust rose in her wake as she pressed forward through the day's heat.

Chapter 42 – Danger in the Cave

Finn, William, and Jesse turned towards the grunting noises. It wasn't any of them and Samuel had retreated to the mouth of the cave to lick his wounds and sulk just out of reach of the sunlight.

Jesse alone recognized the sounds. He had been at the cave when the others were still on their way back from robbing Ruby.

"Oh, did I forget to mention we had a visitor while you were gone?" he said.

William scowled at the ghost, then ran towards his discarded gun belt.

Samuel sprinted into the cave and stopped short between Finn and William. They stood facing a hulking beast, ten feet of bristling fur and muscle. The shaggy beast stood tall on his rear legs. The cave quaked with his deafening roar. He swiped at the air. He snorted and drove forward with powerful strides.

"Get down!" William shouted from behind Finn and Samuel. The two looked with a start as he raised his pistol, taking careful aim at the vision of death that barreled towards them.

He squeezed the trigger. The hot lead missed its mark and grazed the bear's rear haunch.

Finn and Samuel were hurtled to the side as the bear slammed past them. He halted and swung a thick-clawed foot at William. The curled talons ripped through the muscle of his firing arm and knocked his gun free. The pistol fell to the ground out of reach. William shrieked as the beast bore down on him, knocking him on his back.

The bear straddled its front paws on either side of the frightened sheriff. Its wet nose came to within inches from William's face. He held his arms above his head to shield him from the coming blow.

The bear raised his paw to finish William. But the bear could not strike. Finn held tight the beast's great paw.

"Move," Finn shouted. William blinked in disbelief at the sight of the fanged man holding back the full weight of the bear.

The bear turned his attention to the straining vampire as William scrambled to freedom. He held his wounded arm. Sweat poured down his forehead as shock rolled through his body.

A low rumble rattled in the bear's throat as it stared into Finn's black eyes. With little effort, it flung Finn away. The exhausted vampire skidded to a stop, enveloped by a cloud of dust and gravel. The bear bore down on Finn. He shook off his tumble and braced for impact.

Before the bear could reach Finn, it was thrown off balance by Samuel. Samuel had run headlong into its hind quarters. He swiped a hunk out of the animal's hide, splashing the cave floor with blood.

The bear's attention was turned towards its gaping wound. Finn darted around its side and kicked the side of the bear's head. A crack rang across the stone walls of the cave. Finn had dislocated the bear's jaw. The animal slumped over. Finn reached down and pulled at the dazed animal's head. He turned it to the side and exposed its neck. Finn's ears buzzed with the rush of the bear's blood through its veins. He hammered his face into the furry mass of muscle below the bear's limp jaw. The sharp fangs split the thick hide with little effort. The bear struggled while Finn extracted every ounce of strength from it. It hobbled around the room, unable to shake the parasite that drained it.

Samuel watched as his protégé drained the monstrous beast in minutes. If feeding on animals didn't nauseate him, he would have been aroused. Instead, he admired Finn's strength, even so recently revived. With Finn fed, he would not need to sacrifice William as he had planned.

The bear's final heartbeats filled Finn's mouth with the remaining drops of life. He bolted up from his kill, exhilarated and gasping for air. Matted fur clung to his face and mouth. He wiped at his mouth with a pleased look coloring his face, a red streak crossing his cheek and sleeve.

"Feel better?" Samuel asked with a grin.

Finn's smile faded, and the blue color returned to his eyes.

He let go of the limp beast and kicked his leg over the body. A euphoric haze settled over him as he stumbled towards William.

William sat on the gravel floor and clung to his leaking arm. He scanned for a shirt or something to bandage the wound before he bled out.

Finn stood above him. William marveled at the physical change the feeding had brought out in him. Before the bear attack, Finn looked frail. But now, his muscles were filled with vigor and he stood tall. His features were filled in, not shallow as before.

"Thanks for the help back there," William said, his voice strained from pain.

"Is it as bad as it looks?" The concerned vampire knelt next to him.

"I think so."

"Let me see."

"This isn't some trick so you can feed on me too, is it?"

"If I were going to feed on you, you'd be little more than a burp on my breath already." Finn lifted William's bloodied hand and the wound beneath spit out a gush of life. He looked around and saw a rumpled shirt peeking out of his saddle bag. He grabbed the shirt and fashioned a makeshift bandage around the damaged area. William winced at the pains of the tight wrapping that cut off the flow of blood. "That should help keep what's left of you inside."

William felt woozy. He had lost a fair amount of blood and figured he was not long for this world.

Finn stood and turned to Samuel. "You brought him for me too, didn't you?"

"I knew you would need to feed."

Finn lifted him above the ground and with an angry grunt flung the older vampire off into the dark. He considerately aimed him at the cushioned girth of the dead bear. Samuel bounced off the animal and crashed to the dusty ground.

Samuel sprang up. A sharp growl rose in his throat. Finn stared him down. Two alphas vying for dominance...and Finn was winning. Finally, Samuel smiled. "My dear boy. There's no need to get your hackles up. You didn't even need to drain him." He dusted himself off. "Besides, there are more pressing matters we must attend to."

Chapter 43 – Ruby at the Cave

Ruby peered into the cave. She smelled the doused campfire and the stench of rotting meat.

Her eyes adjusted as she stepped into the darkness, the inky black shifting to dark grey as her eyes acclimated. A human body and an animal body lay on the cave floor. She knelt next to what there was of Roy's corpse and waved the buzzing flies away. Then she went to the dead bear. She traced her fingers through its coarse fur.

The sun had dipped below the hills an hour earlier, but until now the horizon had glowed soft yellow. She figured the cave had been vacated mere hours before she had spotted it from the bottom of the valley. That meant her prey had a head start, but she was beginning to close the gap.

She moved towards the mouth of the cave. She took note of the scuffled footprints around the horse tracks.

She would catch them, but since they were on horseback, they had the advantage. She wasn't concerned. She had all the time in the world.

She took a deep, sighing breath and headed in the direction of their tracks.

Chapter 44 – The Ride Back to Thrall

The only solace the silent band took as they raced back towards Thrall was that Ruby had not overtaken them yet. They assumed that meant she was on foot.

It had been two long nights of travel, resting during the highest points of the sunlight to keep the delicate skin of the vampires from bursting into flames. William was still with them, but he was fading. His pale skin was pasty and slick with fevered sweat. His shirt was stained dark brown from the continued loss of blood from the bear attack. They replaced his bandage often, Finn and Samuel taking advantage of the discarded rags to gain a minimal amount of sustenance instead of draining the sheriff.

They settled down for the day in an abandoned mine a few miles from Thrall. They would set out just before the sun went down, but for now they needed to take care of William, who continued to weaken. Samuel worked to convince Finn to finish him and lighten their load so they could make a stand against Ruby without worrying about the dying man. Finn insisted they give the man a chance by taking him back to Thrall. The doctor there could attempt to patch him up and maybe give him a chance at a few more years of life as payment for rescuing Finn in the first place.

"That's disgusting," Jesse said to Samuel as the vampire sucked the red out of a twisted rag coated in William's blood and sweat from the days travel.

Samuel stopped sucking for a moment. He pulled the rag from his mouth. "If I can't feed on him, I'll feed off of him, boy. Keep to yourself." He replaced the rag in his mouth and proceeded to finish his snack.

Jesse shrugged and drifted over to where Finn tended to William. William leaned against the wall of the mine near a fire. Chills had taken control of his weakening body. Finn dabbed the perspiration from his forehead.

"He doesn't look good." Jesse leaned in close to William, who breathed fast and shallow and winced. His pain held him on the edge of sleep and consciousness.

"That's because he's not," Finn said. "Even cauterized, the wound still seeps past the scar tissue and a fever has set in. That bear's claws were far from clean. They dirtied his blood and brought on an infection. Your friend is in a bad way."

Jesse straightened at the word *friend*. "What makes you think he's my friend?"

"You travel with him, don't you? That's usually a sign of friendship, or at least tolerance. He must offer some form of entertainment if you've stuck around instead of floating off to see the world."

"It's funny to pester him, is all. Besides, he's the reason I'm like this."

Finn gave a snort and turned to the pouting spirit.

"Really. You blame the sheriff for this?"

"He kilt me, didn't he?"

"He pulled the trigger, but you are as much to blame for your passing as an instinctual killer. Plus, I'm pretty sure he was ignorant of the conjuring method that stripped you free from him." Finn gave a backward nod toward Samuel, indicating his guilt in partaking in the unbinding spell.

Samuel paid no heed to them as he sucked on the twisted rag.

In his new state of existence, Jesse had found a fresh communion with the world around him. Sounds were new again. Colors were sharp and he could identify every layer of hue that colored the sunrise and sunset. He had reluctantly thought about his predicament as well. His fresh perspectives hadn't stopped him from clinging to the convenient half-truth of how he got to where he was. Just then, the truth of the matter stung him.

"It's not true. William did this."

"Is that why you torment him still, even after your bond was broken?" Finn doused his rag in water from a canteen and a hint of whiskey in an attempt to cool William's fever. He dabbed it across the sheriff's forehead and waited for the stammering boy to answer, but Jesse couldn't.

"Yeah, that's what I thought." Finn set the rag on William's forehead and stood. "You and William had a crossing that was unfortunate. But you have tortured him for your mistake for years. You need to accept your own actions and consequences. That is what being a part of this world is about. It's also what truly binds your spirit to this world. If you ever want to move on to the next plain, you're going to have to figure out how to let go of him." He looked down at William with pity. "Especially since he might not be here much longer."

Finn left the two. Jesse stared down at the sleeping man.

Chapter 45 – The Final Miles

It was time to make the final push to Thrall. Finn and Samuel hoisted William up into his saddle. His face was painted with pained exhaustion. They steadied him as best they could and mounted their horses on either side of him.

"I think it's time I say goodbye." Jesse floated beneath the mounted trio.

"You're not gonna see this through, huh?" Finn said.

"I think you were right. There is a whole world out there and there's nothing really holding me here."

"We must be going if we're going to stay ahead of her, Finn," Samuel said.

Finn turned to him. "Be polite, Samuel. The boy is taking a big step." He turned back to Jesse. "I hope you find more out there than you have riding along with us. Although I must say, it's been an interesting experience getting to know you."

"Likewise, mister. I'd wish you all luck against Ruby, but honestly, I don't much care what happens between y'all." Then with a harsh look towards Samuel: "At least not that one."

Finn chuckled and nodded his final salutation.

The three men trotted off towards Thrall. Jesse floated for a minute, watching them move off. Then he turned and floated up into the air. He stopped about thirty feet up and scanned the landscape for any sign of Ruby. He might not plan on being in Thrall for the final battle, but that did not diminish his curiosity about the dangerous creature giving them chase, and he fancied one last conversation before moving on to the rest of his travels.

Chapter 46 – A Visit to the Doctor

The trio rode into town. William slumped and wheezed in his saddle. The two vampires rode on either side of him in case he began to slip off to the side. They stopped at the doctor's office and secured their horses. The animals snorted in relief.

Finn and Samuel dismounted, but William just swayed in his saddle. Finn rounded his horse and gave the sheriff a gentle tug. His limp body dropped into Finn's arms. Finn carried the gaunt man up the steps and pushed the door open with his foot.

The greying doctor jerked awake in his rocker.

"Sorry for the intrusion," Finn, said, and laid William on the examination table. William groaned.

"No trouble at all." The doctor watched Finn unbutton William's shirt. "What seems to be the...oh, my God. When did this happen?"

"Two days ago, about thirty miles east of here."

"What did this?"

"A bear."

"Anyone else hurt?"

Finn shook his head.

"The sheriff. Jesus, mister. I hardly recognized him."

"I need you to pull him through."

The doctor chewed on the hairs of his overgrown mustache as he considered William's condition. "Probably need to lose the arm."

"I sure would be grateful if you would consider that a last resort."

"He's so far gone I should probably just put a bullet in his head. This is not gonna be pretty and he probably will be sick for quite a while."

Finn jingled his money pouch. "I'll be sure to compensate you."

"That's something we can work out later."

"Okay, then. What do you need?"

"First, I'm gonna need some help. Can you run over to the Braided Pony and find one of the cleaner-looking girls to come lend a hand? Hazel is usually pretty good in these situations."

Finn nodded and hurried off, not eager for the reception he would get from the patrons of his place of death. He would deal with the pitchforks and torches when they came though, just as he had before. For now, William needed help.

Samuel didn't have the same urgency. He settled into the spare rocker on the doctor's porch and whistled.

Chapter 47 – Ruby Reminisces

Ruby could go a long time without food. But the lack of regular blood infusions made her tired and gaunt. It was only two days since she had fed, and already her inner voice ranted and made suggestions of moving on to other pastures, but she was stubborn. She would make them pay for their insolence. She would relish the freshly procured teeth of the two vampires, replenishing her lost supply.

The thought of the feeding made her mouth water and the distant yip of a coyote caught her attention. It had been ages since she had resorted to tasting the flesh of an animal. Humans were the closest she had come to that and at least they provided some playtime before the kill. She decided to ignore the sound.

She wouldn't feed until Thrall. There, or at least on its outskirts, she could take a fresh meal from one of the farms. It had been some time since she had gone up against a vampire who was aware of her. She missed the days when the two species openly vied for dominance. Her kind was hunted down to near-extinction by the hordes of vampires that used to roam the earth. Her kind had grown rare, and the vampire ranks had spread out and grown less organized. This made it easier for her to get around and kill the enemy. They had forgotten what her kind smelled like and she was able to mask her inner monster with the frills and smells of man.

Once, she lured a vampire in under the guise that she was a helpless maiden making her way home in the foggy night. The pungent odor of the hungry creature alerted her to him all the way on the other side of town. She dropped him into a horse trough and scoured the outer layer of filth that coated him.

After that encounter, she took up residency in the local brothels and boardinghouses. She enjoyed making her victims pay for her. She appreciated the attention and the lifestyle. It reminded her of her past, when man worshipped her kind.

Ritual sacrifices were carried out in her honor. The hearts and teeth of her prey cut out on altars by the priests of the land. The humans kept vampires locked up for their monthly tribute. Ruby and her kin lived among them and grew lazy from the ease of the kill. This would lead to their downfall, but while it lasted, she soaked in their adoration and fed on a steady supply.

Her pace quickened as she passed by the burned-out skeleton of the Black Cross Ranch, the first rays of morning staining the horizon purple and orange. On foot it would take her all day and probably part of the night.

She hoped to happen upon a snack soon. If not, there were plenty of souls to quench her thirst with when she arrived in Thrall.

Chapter 48 – William Regains Consciousness

William blinked. The sticky film of sleep and sickness gave his vision a foggy haze. The smell of honey mixed with a wide array of herbs and wild roots struck his nose. The poultice secured to his shoulder burned as it fought his infection. He tried to sit up. His head spun and nausea turned his stomach.

"Whoa there, son." The grizzled doctor stood over him, crumbs of cornbread in his wild mustache. "You need to stay down for a while." He pressed a rough, warm hand on William's bare chest, urging him to lie back down.

"Where am I?"

"You're back in Thrall." The doctor wet a washcloth in a basin next to the table, wrung it out and wet William's cracked lips.

"How long have I been here?" William grabbed at the cloth, took a hard suck to clean some of the moisture out of it, then dabbed the cool rag across his sweat-beaded forehead.

"Not long. About a day."

"Where's Finn?"

"He brought you to me, then took off to the Braided Pony to get a room. I'm pretty sure he is still there. Him and his surly companion haven't so much as ducked their heads out of their rooms all day, as far as I know."

The doctor took the rag again, dipped it in the basin and handed it back to William.

"What time is it?" William lifted his head, risking the nausea. A sharp pain tore through his arm and chest.

"Now, now. That's an angry wound you've got there. I would've taken the arm, but your friend insisted I try whatever I could to keep it. He even gave me a remedy to help cool the infection. Nasty-smelling stuff, but it seems to be doing a good job of sucking out the pus."

William chuckled at the unintended joke the old man made with reference to Finn providing a remedy that sucked.

"What's so funny?" The doctor said.

"Nothing at all. You think you can help me sit up so I can get my bearings?"

"I wouldn't recommend it."

"I'm sure you wouldn't, but I gotta piss like a horse and I doubt you want to be cleaning up after me any more than you have to." William grinned at the old man.

The doctor sighed, stood and moved to William's good side. He helped move William to a sitting position. William worked his feet over the edge of the table and hunched over his knees. His feet dangled inches above the wooden floor.

"Not bad," the doctor said. "You want a bucket or are we gonna try and get you to the outhouse?"

William straightened, ignoring the shooting pains from his shoulder.

"I think I can make it. Can you grab me a crutch?"

"Sure."

"Um..."

"Something else you need, Sheriff?"

"I should probably have a talk with my friends soon. Would you mind going over to the Pony in a bit and checking on them?"

"Will do."

The doctor pulled a dusty crutch from the corner. William slowly maneuvered himself over the edge of the table.

At the door, the doctor stopped and looked back at William. "You, uh, sure you want me to get both of them?"

William looked into the nervous eyes of the old man. "How about you just call on Finn? If the other one comes along, that's fine, but no need for you to go bother him in his room."

The doctor pressed his lips together and headed off.

William picked up the linen shirt draped over the back of the man's chair. He passed his good arm into the sleeve and slipped the other side over his bandaged shoulder. He began the arduous trek to the outhouse. Every step hurt, but at least he was alive.

The thought of being glad at his predicament made him smile. He was injured, aligned with two murderous creatures that viewed him as food, and a third monster was on her way to dismantle his town, board by board in search of the villains that stole her fountain of youth.

What a place to be, he thought.

Chapter 49 — Plots and Plans

"What do you mean, run?" Samuel despised William's cowardice. He should have eaten the man while they were still on the trail.

"I don't think you should fight her right now. Not in my town, at least." William straightened up, supported by his crutch.

"But we have to make a stand at some point and there's no better place then here."

"Again, Samuel, I'm telling you we ought to run."

"The problem is Ruby's sure to be close by. She'll either meet us here or tear up the town to find out which way we went. We should be here to prevent that at the very least, wouldn't you say?"

"And what then? If you win, what does the town owe you?"

"Is that what you're worried about? I'm sure we can come to some sort of agreement, especially if the townsfolk provide a service that proves useful in taking Ruby out."

"All right, since you put it that way, I'll hear you out. What do you propose?" William shuffled to a chair and dropped his sore body down to hear Samuel's proposition.

"First, we need to figure out just how far away she is. Sending out a scout or two would help us gauge how much time we have to get ready. Second, we enlist any townsfolk that can help to weaken her once she arrives. And third, we turn this town into a shooting gallery that funnels Ruby to us."

"And what do we do with her then?" Finn asked.

Samuel turned to his old friend. "We take her apart, isn't that obvious? One piece at a time." He flicked his tongue across his lips, hunger on his face. "William, can you assemble your people so we can tell them what's coming?"

William's head dropped with an exhausted sigh, then lifted, his eyes darkened with the idea of leading the townsfolk to the slaughter. "How much are you gonna tell them about what's coming?"

"Well, it won't be pleasant, not even in a place like this, but I have an idea of how to get their attention."

Chapter 50 - Town Meeting

Neither Samuel nor Finn liked the idea of preaching to the masses in the local house of the Lord. Neither was a fan of the Christian Savior and their kind was notoriously allergic to many of the religious tools involved. That left the Braided Pony as the next largest room in town.

The townsfolk assembled on the second floor of the Braided Pony to hear the proposal of the two outsiders. William had put the word out that a great danger was coming and he needed every available hand to attend.

The rafters hummed with rumors. Drinks were on hand to calm people's nerves. William was known as an eccentric drunk, not an alarmist. Since he returned with his injury though, his eyes seemed clearer and he almost seemed like a sheriff again.

The room was filled with the usual clientele, as well as the churchgoing farmers and teetotalers. William, and Finn kept Earl company behind the bar.

William turned to Finn. "I think that's about it, and honestly, I'm surprised we got this many."

"This is good," Finn said. "It's up to Samuel now."

"Yeah, that's what I'm afraid of. Do you have any idea what he's planning?"

"I never do, but we best get started. Why don't you get their attention and let him take it from there?"

William nodded. Still feeling weak from his wounds, he stepped up on a stool and nearly fell off again. He got his balance and raised his hand to quiet the crowd. The murmurs continued.

"May I have your attention?" William said. He hammered his crutch on the bar top. The sharp crack resonated through the room and the crowd hushed.

"Thank you." He cleared his throat. "I know you all are not used to meeting on such short notice. I appreciate your time."

"You can appreciate my time by paying for an hour with Mary Elizabeth," a brown-toothed farmhand shouted. The room erupted with laughter and a chorus of lewd retorts.

"Baby, the day you last an hour your service is free." Mary Elizabeth fired back as the crowd whooped and hollered their approval of her take down.

William smacked the bar again to quiet the room. "Pretty sure none of us have enough money to convince Mary Elizabeth to take on that task, Bob." The room laughed down the heckler. "Now seriously, folks. We have a problem coming our way and I need to ask your help."

"What kinda problem got you spooked, Sheriff?" The preacher said, craning his neck to see William around the crowd of parishioners.

"The kind that will take all of us to clean up whether

we want to or not." The room hummed concern and quieted again. "I want to introduce everyone to my travel companions." He gestured to his right. "This is Finn. Some of you might remember him from the brawl in here about a week ago."

The crowd objected.

"I thought he was dead."

"Yeah! Didn't something happen to Ruby because of him?"

"What are you trying to pull, Sheriff?"

William held up his hands to quiet them. "Finn here did take down three men about a week ago. I decided he was acting in self-defense and let him go. After that he enjoyed a night here at the Braided Pony with Ruby. The next morning, we found a mutilated body in Ruby's room."

"Who was it?"

Finn stepped forward. "That dead body was mine."

The room exploded in a mixture of laughter and gasps. "Whatchoo gettin' at Sheriff? This some kinda witchcraft or trickery?"

"What happened in that room is only part of the reason everyone is here tonight. Finn coming back is the least of our problems. In fact, he and his friend are probably the only ones that can take care of the problem that's on its way as we speak."

The crowd roared with questions and shouts of demons. William shouted for quiet, waving his good arm and the crutch to bring everyone back to his attention. It was the smack of the wooden slat door though, that turned heads and quieted the uproar.

Samuel strode into the saloon, leading a mule. He guided it to the center of the room and stood in front of William. William looked questioningly at Finn, who answered with a shrug. Then Finn dropped his head in disbelief as he contemplated his old mentor's intentions. He pulled at William's shirt to get him to step down and out of the way.

Samuel looked around the room, drawing the gaze of every person.

He bowed his head theatrically. The animal snorted, agitated. It quivered and brayed, searching for an escape. When Samuel raised his head again his eyes were black as night. He opened his mouth wide. His horrific fangs were extended and glistened with a slick layer of drool. The crowd shrieked as he slammed his face into the mule's neck. The poor creature struggled to break free of Samuel's deadly hold. He dug his sharp nails into the animal's sides and tore into its flesh. A red mist painted the boots and pant legs of the nearest bystanders. The crowd scrambled back from the terrifying display of power.

Samuel unlatched his mouth from the mule. He laughed and pulled outward with his arms. The animal's rib cage split open. He let the dead thing drop to the blood- and beer-stained floorboards.

Unfazed, William and Finn shook their heads at the heavy-handed display.

Samuel raised his bloody hands as if he needed to silence the already terror-stricken crowd.

"Friends. This sacrifice was to show you what's in store for your town once the beast arrives."

A portly farmhand stood out and pointed to the twitching mess on the floor. "The only beast I know of is standing in front of us right now!"

"This was extreme, I'll admit." Samuel burped. "Excuse me. But imagine the carnage that a creature ten times my strength can cause. Finn and I are greater than humans as far as strength and appetite go, but the creature on its way here is stronger and blood thirstier than the two of us combined."

"What do you want from us," someone shouted from the back of the crowd.

"I expect you want to live to see another sunrise, ma'am." Samuel looked around the room. "Am I right?"

People grumbled, but nodded.

"Good. Now, your sheriff is going to explain what needs to happen and how we can save as many of you as possible while ridding this world of a vile creature. William, you may take the stage, as it were."

Finn helped a grey-faced William back up onto his stool.

"Right," William said. "So, what we need is pretty simple, but not easy. First, we need volunteers to ride out and scout. After that we need to prep the town with as much firepower and bodies as we can muster before she gets here."

"She?" A befuddled farmer stepped forward, chuckling at the insinuation. "Did you say she? I thought you said there was a monster on its way."

"There is. And her name is Ruby."

Chapter 51 – Jesse and Ruby

Jesse floated above the desert, scanning for Ruby for most of the day and into the night. At last, he caught a glimpse of her small figure trudging in the direction of Thrall. He lowered himself down about a mile in front of her and waited.

She came into view and the boy catalogued everything he could about her. He figured she would be dolled up in a nice dress with feathers in her hair and fancy bangles galore. These were the images conjured by his adolescence when him and his friends had joked around about the girls who took up at the Braided Pony.

As she neared, he caught a very different picture of just who she was and how far she had traveled. Her purpose drove her to walk with her head bowed and focused on the horizon. Her satin dress and heeled boots had seen better days. Miles of chase had tattered the hem and made much of the embroidery and sewn-in sparkles come loose, giving her a patchwork look to her once polished appearance. Her hair flew in all directions with thick locks dangling, loosened from the tight formation she had started with. The only feather left was stripped bare by the weather as she had trekked after her prey.

Ruby did not see him at first, so fixed she was on her vengeful steps. As she came to within mere feet of him, she slowed and struggled to focus on the transparent form floating in front of her.

Jesse waved at her.

"Hello," he said. "Ruby, is it?"

"It is. But I don't know you."

"My name is Jesse." He extended his hand to shake, then remembered that she would not be able to touch him. "You look a bit different than I expected."

"You expected me? Are you friends with anyone I might know?" Her inquisitive tone changed to one of annoyance.

"Oh, yes. I'm friends with the sheriff."

"Ah, yes." She relaxed a bit as the pieces fell into place. "Are you what's been troubling that man every night?"

"I am, or at least I was. It's hard to explain."

"Why don't you try? I'm guessing that if you're here, they're just up the way a bit so I'm in no hurry and could use a bit of a break myself." She moved toward a dried-out log and sat down to hear Jesse's story.

He skipped over most of his childhood. But he painted a picture of his quest for manhood at the end of a gun barrel that ended with the beginning of William's nightly walks.

Jesse talked of his travels with William, Samuel, Roy, and eventually the resurrected Finn.

"Quite a story," Ruby said. "Now what is there you can tell me about the reception they've got planned for me in Thrall?"

"Not much. The townsfolk are with them, so you get to deal with them first. What you really need to look for is the three of them holed up in the Braided Pony."

"Of course, they would be," she said, and laughed.

"I'm pretty sure they won't be upset at me tellin' you all this since you probably already figured most of it out."

"Sort of. So, what does this world have in store for you now that you're no longer stuck in your nightly gunfights with the sheriff?"

"I thought maybe you could help me out a bit with that."

Ruby stood and dusted off her ragged dress. "What could I do for you? Pretty sure I can't free you by sucking you down like a shot of whiskey."

"I mostly wondered if you had ever encountered someone, er, something like me in your travels."

Ruby thought for a moment. "Not quite like you. Most spirits tend to be tied to a place or a thing, sometimes even people. But you've been freed from your prison without the advantage of the portal taking you into the next world."

"Yeah...I saw that with Roy, but there was no way to follow him."

"The best I can offer you is the same as Samuel, I guess. To point you in a direction and see you on your way."

"A bit anticlimactic isn't it?"

"So was your passing."

Her words hurt. He dropped his head and Ruby began to walk on in the direction of Thrall.

"If it's any consolation," Ruby called back, "if you decide to stick around, you should be able to see quite the show. Not to mention the end of Samuel, who put you in such a precarious situation instead of sending you off into the ether. That would have been the merciful thing to do."

"I'm pretty sure you are mostly right. But I wouldn't underestimate Finn."

She stopped short and turned back towards him. "I must admit, I'm intrigued by his return. He was one of my tastier meals. How do you suppose he will taste to me under our present circumstances?"

Jesse shuddered at the monstrous hints in her broad smile.

Still, he reminded himself, there were things she couldn't possibly know...

"I'm pretty sure you'll have a spirited battle," he said, "but I wouldn't count on the idea of you continuing on in this world when all of this is done." He turned away from her and moved off towards the darkening horizon. "Curious, though."

"What's that, sweetie?"

"What's *your* next destination once they rip your head from its perch? Do you think the bright light will call you up? Or will you be dragged away screaming and mewing like a frightened lamb for the roast on Hell's coals?"

Ruby watched as Jesse's opaque figure hardened in the cooling sky and he disappeared into the dusk.

Chapter 52 – The Scouting Party

"Do you believe that shit back at the saloon?" Brady asked.

"Believe it? I believe I haven't puked that much since the time Jimbo was in charge of dinner out on the trail." Bob felt a slick sweat creep its way across his forehead at the memory of the mule being disemboweled.

The two cowhands had volunteered as scouts. They agreed to do it in part to distance themselves from the monsters that were back in town, and also to get a peek at what had such powerful creatures scared enough to enlist an entire town to take down one lady.

"Don't remind me," Brady said. "Anyway, do you believe any of this?"

"I know, it's crazy ain't it?"

"That don't even start to cover it."

The two rode in silence for a few minutes, heading east on the fastest horses the town could spare in search of Ruby.

The rest of the town rearranged the main street into a shooting gallery. The alleys and side streets were blocked up to funnel traffic to the Braided Pony.

The two scouts trotted through the evening without a sign of her. Both had had intimate moments with her. They had inhaled deeply of her sweet floral scents and laughed at her bawdy jokes. They had felt her bring them to a panting finish and enjoyed the soft warmth of her breath against their necks afterward. Not that they held any loyalty towards her. But they couldn't believe she was capable of any of the things the monsters at the saloon had described.

No way someone with such a petite frame could be a party to such violence, let alone its instigator. That was why the two had taken up the task; they hoped to confront the woman themselves.

"It just can't be true." Brady shook his head.

Bob slowed his horse to a stop. Brady halted and directed his horse around to face his friend.

"You're probably right," Bob said, "but you saw what that guy did back at the bar. That was unnatural...and he says he's afraid."

"So, should we warn her if we see her or just do what we're supposed to?" Brady asked.

Bob chewed on his lip nervously. His horse snorted and its eyes darted back and forth through the moonlit night. "I don't know. We should prob—"

He was cut off as a dark figure leapt onto the back of his horse. Ruby wrapped her vice-like arms around Bob and pulled him close, forcing the wind from his lungs.

She brought her chin up over his shoulder, her lips just below his earlobe. "Hey, lover. Been a while." She flicked her tongue at his ear, then bit it off and spat it out. The confused horse spun in circles.

"Holy shit!" Brady drew his gun and pulled the hammer back. He aimed towards the two figures. "Let him go!"

Ruby laughed; her heels dug into the sides of the horse to steady him. "How about I give you a choice? You can have a head start and leave your friend here with me for a little play time..."

"Or?"

"Or I feed on you both." Ruby's teeth glinted in the moonlight.

"Help me," Bob pleaded, reaching toward his friend.

"I'm sorry, buddy." Brady uncocked and slid his gun back into its leather sheath.

"Good choice," Ruby said. "But don't leave empty-handed."

Brady heard a yelp from Bob and was hit in the chest with a wet, heavy thump. He juggled the slippery projectile and looked down into Bob's blinking eyes. He screamed, reared up his horse and raced back towards Thrall, leaving Bob's head on the ground.

"See you soon, lover." Ruby drank from the pooling spring of Bob's neck. The body squirmed in her arms as she replenished her strength from her journey. She would have preferred the full meal the two men would have provided, but Bob was enough for now.

She drank him dry and dropped his body to the ground. She shifted forward in the saddle and calmed the horse. Then she set off at a trot, the horse stepping over Bob's corpse, carrying its new owner back to town.

Chapter 53 — The Scout Returns

Brady raced back to Thrall; the dawn chased him into the streets. His horse was slick with sweat and nearly collapsed as he brought it to a halt. He flung himself to the ground and scrambled off to report his run-in with Ruby. He burst into the sheriff's office and dropped to his knees, panting and grunting from his hard ride.

William shot up in bed. His shoulder burned and the interruption threw him half out of his cot. "What is it, Brady? Where's Bob?" He blinked the sleep from his eyes and cradled his wounded arm in his lap.

"Dead," the farmhand said. "Something snuck up on us outside of town." He slumped over, tears mingled with the sweat and dirt on his face.

"It's okay, Brady. How far out were you when she got Bob?"

"About...ten miles...or so."

"Did she take off after you?"

"No, I don't think so. I tore ass outta there, but I didn't look back to see if she was following me or not."

William nodded and rose from his cot. "You done good." He walked up next to Brady and placed a hand on his shoulder. "I'm sorry about your pal. Why don't you go get a bit of rest and some grub? It's gonna be a long day."

Brady wiped at his messy face with the back of his sleeve and stood up next to William. He slowly turned and moved towards the door.

"I'll kill her for what she did to Bob," he said, then stepped outside to put away his horse.

Under his breath, William said, "I doubt it. But I appreciate your enthusiasm."

"You know he's gonna die, don't you?" Jesse had been quiet since they returned to Thrall, so his sudden appearance startled William.

"Kid, we will probably all die in one way or another by the end of this day."

"So why not just run?"

"Because that's not what I do."

"Sure, it is. You've been running into a whiskey bottle for years. What's the difference between that and just getting on your horse and hightailing it outta here?"

"I'm not in the mood for your shit today, Jesse." William walked past the apparition and splashed water on his face at the water basin.

"Okay, so you don't run, but you're not exactly giving the other folks much of an option, either. How is that right?"

"We told them what to expect. They had every opportunity to pull up stakes. So if they hang around for what's comin', then that's on them. All I can do at this point is give them the best opportunity to fight for their home."

He dried his face with an old shirt. He rolled his injured shoulder to gauge its mobility. It popped and whined with pain, but the infection had retreated and he could almost lift his arm again.

"You're full of shit, you know that?" Jesse taunted him.

He spun on the ghost. "You're not wrong, son, now git outta here and bug someone else for a bit. I wanna get dressed and you ain't nearly purdy enough for me to be excited about sharing that moment with you."

With a frown, Jesse glided away and disappeared through the far wall.

Chapter 54 – Final Preparations

The corridor into town blew cold with the chill of evening as the sun dipped below the surrounding hills. Nervous townsfolk peered into the distance for signs of Ruby. The horse she had stolen had been spotted an hour ago about a mile outside of town. Inexperienced shooters breathed shallowly and hoped their anxious twitches would not set off the triggers of their weapons until it was time for action.

The doctor had reluctantly cleared William for action. The majority of the town's children and older inhabitants hunkered down in the basement of the church.

Most of the town's shooters were positioned at second-floor windows or on top of roofs overlooking the main thoroughfare.

William, Finn, and Samuel waited inside the Braided Pony. Finn and Samuel shared a bottle of whiskey at a center table. William looked down on them from Ruby's old perch on the second-floor landing.

Finn asked, "How wise do you think she is to our plan?" Then drained a shot of whiskey.

"Wise enough." Samuel filled Finn's glass and threw back a shot of his own. "I don't think the gauntlet outside will scare her off. If anything, she'll use it to take out as many of those hicks as she can before reaching us for the real fight."

Samuel reached down to his hip. Finn's eyes narrowed as Samuel pulled out the wooden blade that Finn had used to kill him. Samuel twisted the long blade, admiring its craftsmanship. He smiled at Finn, then set the weapon on the table.

"I got this from William after the bear attack," he said. "I thought you might like it back for when we face Ruby. Assuming we take her out, what do you propose happens after the dust settles?"

"Well, if we're still moving at the end of it, then I will shove that blade of mine straight through your heart." Finn drained his shot glass and stood. "Again."

He took the knife and headed outside.

The purple of night settled over Thrall.

Chapter 55 - Showdown in Thrall

Clem wiped sweat from his brow. He stared down the barrel of his Winchester to the street below. He wanted to get the first shot in to reap a hero's rewards with the ladies at the Braided Pony. His post on the roof of the mercantile was the perfect vantage point.

"Evening, Clem."

The hairs on the back of his neck stood on end as Ruby's sultry voice tickled his ear.

His yelp was cut short as Ruby slashed a curved talon across his throat. His life spilled onto the floor of the roof where he stood. He pawed at his sticky wet throat and collapsed, ushered into deathly sleep by his own gurgled lullaby.

The other sentries missed the show as they watched the street. Ruby backed away from the edge and made her way down the back stairs.

Bart and Carson stared intently through the

darkening evening, down the avenue, awaiting Ruby to stroll into range. The two farmers had the practiced aim of lifelong hunters.

Ruby took off her shoes and ascended the stairs of the boarding house where Bart and Carson were posted. The only sound the two men heard was the plop of saliva on the porch behind them as she unfurled her tongue and severed Bart's spinal cord at the base of his skull. Bart slumped over and his rifle dropped to the ground.

She turned her attention to Carson. She clamped her massive jaws around his head. Her rows of teeth bored into his skull. She dragged him off the balcony and delivered her final crushing bite out of sight of the shooters across the way.

Tom and Sam, stationed on the roof opposite of Carson and Bart, had missed Ruby's entrance but heard Carson's gun hit the deck. They shifted their attention from the empty street to the action across the street.

"Jesus!" Tom brought his rifle up to his shoulder. He fired, startling Sam back from his shocked state.

The two men opened fire on their invisible target. The doorway erupted into dust and splinters as they emptied their ammunition into the side of the opposite building.

In the Braided Pony, Samuel and Finn looked at each other. "I guess she's here." Samuel said, throwing back the last of his whiskey in a single swallow.

"Do you think they'll get her before she makes it here?" William called down from the upper landing, shaking off the grog of boredom and feeling the tingle of adrenaline with each gunshot that echoed through the streets.

"I doubt it." Finn stood and checked the loaded chambers of his six-shooter. With a flick of his wrist, the loaded chamber locked back in place.

William unholstered a pistol and placed it, hammer primed, into his weaker hand. He drew and cocked his other pistol and aimed at the slatted swinging door, awaiting Ruby's grand entrance.

As soon as the gunfire erupted, Ruby finished off Carson and dashed out of the room, chased away by the onslaught of bullets. She was a blur as she dashed down the stairs. She darted out the front door and across the street to where the two frantic shooters unloaded their arsenal.

They didn't notice her cross the street, but they heard and felt the building shift as she crashed through the front door. The splintered door hurtled through the store. It smashed through glass display cases and sent sweets and sundries in every direction. Ruby dashed up the stairs toward the roof. The two men screamed as their rifles clicked empty. They panicked and scrambled to reload.

Ruby launched through the door to the roof. Tom and Sam fumbled with their half-loaded weapons, but she was on them before they could get off a single round. She took Sam to the ground. Only his rifle separated her talons from his chest. Tom pulled back the hammer on his rifle. Alerted by the sharp click of the hammer, Ruby lifted Sam up and held him between her and the barrel of Tom's gun.

Sam screamed as the buckshot tore through his back and he fell dead into Ruby's arms. She laughed as the horrific realization splashed across Tom's face that he had shot his friend. She tossed Sam's body at him. He was pinned underneath his friend's dead weight, unable to reload.

Ruby stood over him. His high-pitched scream tore through the night air as she stuck two glistening talons into his eyes. He was dead in an instant.

Planks of wood next to her head exploded from gunfire. Slivers of wood, hot from the explosion, ripped into the side of her face. She wiped at the wound and lapped at the drops of blood from her hand.

A man with two six-shooters stood below her on the balcony, readying his next shot. He fired just as she leapt into the air. He continued to fire, following her arc of flight. She landed in front of him. He steadied his aim and pulled his triggers. The two shots hit their mark.

The bullets tore into her chest, knocking Ruby backwards. She smiled as his guns clicked empty. "Not bad, boy. You are the only one who's managed to get me yet."

He fumbled with his pistols. He dropped one and searched his belt for fresh bullets.

Ruby stood. She looked down at her wounds. She took her finger and thumb and dug her sharp talons into one of the sticky holes oozing black. She plucked loose the soft lead bullet that had flattened upon entry. She held it up to examine it and smiled. The terrified man fiddled with the empty chambers of his pistol.

Ruby flicked the warm, slippery bullet at the man, so that it richocheted off his forehead. He winced in surprise, and in the time it took to blink, Ruby had shoved her hand into his stomach. She lifted the screaming man off the ground. He pounded on her arm in a frenzy. She wound back and slammed him into the support beam of the building's awning. His spine snapped in her grip. She let him fall.

She looked across the street at the final three shooters. With a wink and a kiss, she backed away into the recess of the boarding house.

The shooters readied their weapons. Jeb kept his aim on the street, while Daniel and Caleb trained their weapons on the doorway.

She ran around the outside of the town while they watched the street. She entered the back door of the town's newspaper office. She crept through the building and snuck out the front, just under the second-floor balcony where the men were stationed. She slunk to the side of the building and climbed. She came up even with the overhang and peeked around the corner. She saw Jeb looking out over the street while the other two had their attention on the room where they expected her to come from.

She continued her ascent and pulled herself onto the roof. She positioned herself directly above them. She leaned out over the edge and extended her tongue. She coiled it around Jeb's neck and reeled him in. He flew from his spot and dropped his rifle on the floor and the gun went off.

Caleb and Daniel turned to the empty space where their friend had been. A thump above them on the roof signaled the quick end he had met as his disembodied head dropped from Ruby's mouth.

She dropped down to the overhang, between the two cowhands, Jeb's lifeless head, his eyes still twitching, clutched in her hand.

"Heads-up, boys!" she said and swung the head into Caleb's face so hard he fell dead where he stood.

Daniel screamed and fired too late. Ruby flew in through the window next to him, her claws extended, and sliced at him as she moved past. His severed arm dropped along with his gun. His eyes bulged at the sight of his disembodied arm. He fumbled for his pistol at his hip with his other arm, but it was on the wrong side. Ruby stepped forward and slashed at him again. He slumped to the side, the muscles in his right leg peeking out from his reddening pants. He slipped in his own blood, still trying to draw his other gun.

Ruby hovered over him. He screamed and she silenced him, tearing his throat out.

She shifted back to her fully human form as she made her way to the Braided Pony. She smoothed the wrinkles from her tattered and blood-splattered corset and pushed through the batwing doors into the saloon, hungry for her final challenge.

Chapter 56 - Dance of the Dead

"Ruby," Finn said.

"Finn. I must say you've looked worse." Ruby winked and walked over to the bar.

She found a bottle of whiskey and popped the cork from its mouth. "You're not still sore about how we left things, are you?" She took a hard pull from the bottle.

"Just a bit. But you did break my heart, after all." Finn smiled at her, remembering the moments before she literally tore his heart out.

"I see you brought a playmate this time. You gotta pay extra for him to watch." She held the whiskey bottle by the neck and drank from it as she came back from behind the bar.

"You'll be the one covering the tab this time, Ruby."

Finn and Samuel pushed out from their chairs and faced off with the innocent façade of the creature that taunted them.

Ruby smirked. "Do I make you boys nervous? Little ol' me, frightening two such strong, tough men like you?"

"Maybe just a little," Samuel said.

"Now you, I don't know, but I've seen how incapable you can be, haven't I?"

Samuel didn't like to be reminded of his fight with Finn.

Ruby giggled, took another drink and looked up at William on the second floor. "And you, Sheriff. How are your evening walks these days, sweetie?"

William ignored the taunt, keeping his pistols on Ruby.

"So are you boys planning on double-teaming me or are we going to do this one at a time?"

Finn and Samuel grabbed their table and flung it at her. It crashed into her, smashing her whiskey bottle into her face. Finn ran forward, firing his weapon into the table. His bullets ripped through the dry wood and into Ruby.

Samuel followed right behind him. The two landed on the table, splitting it in two, Ruby underneath, the shattered remnants of her whiskey bottle protruding from her face, her hands pinned beneath the table halves and a vampire on either side.

Ruby struggled under their weight. She raged from the sting of hot lead in her belly and chest, and the warmth of the broken glass cutting into her face. She screamed as the two emptied their guns into her. Finn clicked empty first, tossed his gun to the side and reached for the wooden blade at his hip.

Ruby assumed her demonic appearance. The whiskey

bottle in her face flew free from the swift change. Her slicing tongue whipped out and knocked Samuel's guns from his grip. Venomous talons hammered through the table. Samuel flew out of harm's way, relieving the weight on her left arm. She swung the table half at Finn, knocking him off and into the side of the bar, the sound of splintering wood filled the room. William calmly waited for his turn to add to the fight.

With the two vampires knocked free, he seized his chance. He took aim at her left leg. He emptied the pistol in his weak arm first. Shot after shot ripped into Ruby's thigh. She pulled the table half up to protect her body and head.

Finn and Samuel stayed back until William had emptied both barrels. He dropped his left pistol and secured his other pistol under his arm to reload. He took slow steps down the stairs as the vampires went to work.

Ruby flailed, only one leg attached so she couldn't get up. Her left arm was still clamped to the table half, her claws stuck in the wood grain. She pushed her right arm free and worked to pry her left arm loose.

Finn recovered from his meeting with the mangled bar. He ran towards her, his wooden blade held high. Samuel ran to her trapped hand and slammed it down underneath the broken table. He dodged the swiping strikes from her free hand. Finn swung and tore her free arm from her body. She whipped her tongue back and forth and managed quick, short slices, painful, but not debilitating for her two opponents who were quickly taking the upper hand.

Finn reared up again for another strike. He brought

the blade down on Ruby's fanged maw. The crunch of jawbone and the pop of cartilage and connective tissue pierced the air as he sawed away, bisecting her head. He thrust his weight down on the blade and put all his strength into his efforts. He rocked back and forth, dodging the frantic tongue while Samuel pinned her other arm down.

Her bones gave way and his blade cut through to the floorboards. Ruby's angry eyes went dim and the flailing tongue dropped limp across her chest. Her muscles relaxed underneath Samuel's weight.

"Do you think that did it?" William came down the stairs, his freshly loaded gun trained on Ruby. A black pool spread outward from the severed head and limbs they had taken during their fight.

"I doubt it." Finn, painted in Ruby's insides, looked up. He got to his feet and shook from the nerve-jangling effects of his exertions.

He walked to the bar, found a bottle of clear liquor and yanked the cork from the home-brewed spirit with his teeth. He spit it across the room, took a hard pull, then walked to Ruby's body. He emptied the bottle out on her. William walked over to a lamp that glowed yellow on the wall. He lifted up the lamp chimney and plucked the candle from it. He looked to his companions for their approval, then dropped the candle to the ground where a pool of the high-proof alcohol fumed up from the floor. Ruby was engulfed in yellow and orange flames.

The fire spread quickly and soon the saloon was a crackling inferno. The three strode out into the evening, a plume of smoke trailing behind them as the Braided

Pony lit the night. Thrall would never be the same without the saloon.

William didn't believe that was necessarily a bad thing, though. It would only be a matter of time before another establishment took its place. That was the order of things.

Finn, Samuel, and William watched the building burn. They only hoped that beheading and fire would be enough to end Ruby.

In all his decades walking the west, Samuel had never encountered such a creature. He had a hard time reconciling that she was the only one out there, but he had all the hope in the world that she was the last one he would run across.

"It's time for you to be moving on, Samuel," William said. He purposefully stood between the two vampires, not wishing for any more violence to be enacted this evening. "You too, Finn."

"You don't think this is over, do you?" Samuel said.

"It's over enough and I don't want either of you in my town anymore." William turned to Samuel and stared him down.

"You know I can take you and not feel either way about it, don't you?" Samuel said.

"I do. And I don't give a damn what you feel."

Finn put a hand on William's good arm, gently holding him back. "We will go, Sheriff. Won't we, Samuel?"

Samuel relented. "Of course." He winked at William, then said to Finn: "Which way shall we go, my friend?"

"Just know that whatever direction you go, I'll be

going the opposite."

"After all this, you still have it in your mind to leave me?"

"I do."

"Fine. Be a petulant child. I'll find others again."

"If I hear that you have, I'll hunt you down myself, Samuel," William said. "Now git."

Samuel hesitated, then nodded and turned toward the livery to find a horse.

"And Samuel," William added, "don't come back to my town ever again, or I will finish what Finn here couldn't."

Samuel gave a cocky smile, tipped his hat and walked away.

A minute later, William and Finn stood together and watched the elder vampire ride out into the night.

William turned to Finn. "It's your turn."

"I know."

"I hold no ill will towards you, Finn. But bad seems to follow you around and I've had just about enough of these things to last me a lifetime."

"I don't blame you, Sheriff. I will go. And don't worry. I don't plan on coming back this way."

William nodded respectfully.

Finn held his hand out to the sheriff, then remembered his shaking hand was still injured. He switched hands and the two men shook goodbye. Finn went off to the livery and found a horse that would suit him for a long ride. The night was young enough that he could get a good distance between him and Samuel before the light peeked out above the hills. He climbed up onto the horse and gave a gentle kick to its side. They went westward.

William watched him ride away.

The rest of the night he stood by, waiting for the flaming building to collapse. By the time dawn winked hello, it had turned to cinders.

After a while, he went to the church and brought the rest of the townsfolk back to the world of the living. The next day was spent mourning and cleaning up the rotting corpses that Ruby had left in her wake.

When the smoke cleared and the heat abated, William ventured into the rubble of the black skeleton of the Braided Pony to ensure Ruby had gone up with the timbers. The heat had been intense enough to burn away or melt most anything that was in the building when it lit, so he had little expectation that anything would have made it through the fire without being turned to ash.

He kicked through the refuse and came to her final resting spot. Within the remnants and embers, he could make out the shape of bones, laid out where she had been. The flesh had been stripped clean off and nothing but her ashen skeleton were left, cracked and fractured from the heat of the fire.

He tapped the toe of his boot to her burnt femur. The brittle bones dropped to dust and were shuffled away by the gentle morning breeze. Ruby was in the wind and scattered to the reaches of the earth. William was sure there was nothing that could bring her back. There was not even enough of anything to dilute into a tea like she had planned to do with Finn.

With a sigh of relief, he walked back to his sheriff's

station to rest and wash off before facing the next stage of clean-up that would clear out the refuse of what had been the Braided Pony.

The End

About the Author

Author and musician John Dover began his writers' journey with his Jazz-Noir, Johnny Scotch, novellas and comic book series. John has been a contributing author in a number of horror anthologies (*Tales From the Braided Pony*, *100*  *Word Horrors*, *Carnival of Horrors*, *Tenebrous* and more) and also released his own trumpet method book in 2019. Outside of his writing, John is a professional musician, spending his time performing and recording with a wide variety of artists along with teaching and performing as a guest artist and clinician for schools. John lives in Portland, Oregon with his wife, Jessica, a respected Spanish interpreter and translator.

You can find more information on John Dover's music and writing at the following links:
www.readjohndover.com
www.johndmusic.com
www.breakingrulespublishing.com
www.stitchedsmilepublications.com
www.amazon.com/author/johndover
www.facebook.com/johndoverauthor
twitter - @jscotchjustice
Instagram - @johnnyscotchjustice

Special Thanks

To my wife, Jessica. Your talent and bright spirit inspire me every day to be the best version of myself. No amount of words can express how lucky I am to have you in my life.

Thanks to Chuck Anderson and Alucard Press for helping me bring The Braided Pony to life nearly 4 years ago in my first blood-soaked vision of the Wild West.

Thanks to my editor, Charles Austin Muir. Your keen eye and our late-night scotch sessions truly helped to deliver the lean, mean, blood sucking machine that is Once Upon A Fang in the West.

Finally, thanks to Benjamin Gorman and Viveca Shearin of Not A Pipe Publishing for taking a chance on this crazy Spaghetti Western-Horror mashup.

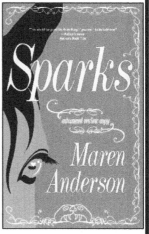

Made in the USA
Monee, IL
08 May 2021

68064951R00132